BLACK LOTUS

BY K'WAN

Published by Akashic Books
©2014 K'wan

Hardcover ISBN-13: 978-1-61775-265-0
Paperback ISBN-13: 978-1-61775-266-7
Library of Congress Control Number: 2013956779

Infamous Books
www.infamousbooks.net

Akashic Books
Twitter: @AkashicBooks
Facebook: AkashicBooks
E-mail: info@akashicbooks.com
Website: www.akashicbooks.com

Also available from Infamous Books

The White House
by JaQuavis Coleman

Swing
by Miasha

H.N.I.C.
by Albert "Prodigy" Johnson with Steven Savile

Ritual
by Albert "Prodigy" Johnson and Steven Savile
(forthcoming)

BLACK
LOTUS

PROLOGUE

IT WAS NEARLY MIDNIGHT BEFORE FATHER FLEMING was able to finally stop and take a breath. It had been a busy day at the church, with two funerals and a confessional that went on for nearly an hour. A woman had committed adultery and was carrying her lover's baby. She was terrified that her husband would leave her and wanted to abort the fetus rather than telling him. Father Fleming was quick to remind her that abortion was murder and a sin. They sat and talked for a long while, exploring alternatives. She eventually agreed to bring her husband in the next day to see Father Fleming, hoping that would make breaking the news easier. He promised her that he and the Lord would do all they could to walk them through the troubled waters. Doing the Lord's work was often tiring, but the joy that filled Father Fleming's heart with every soul he helped made it worth it.

A soft breeze tickled the back of Father Fleming's neck. He cast a glance over his shoulder and saw that the front door of the church was ajar, flapping in the evening wind. It struck him as odd because he was sure he had closed it before sweeping the empty aisles. It seemed like the older he got the more forgetful he was becoming. Using the edge of the bench he was sitting on to push to his feet, Father Fleming shuffled to the door and closed it, this time sliding the lock into place. With his chores done, he was ready to retire for the night.

When Father Fleming began heading back to the room he kept in the rear of the church, something in the middle of the aisle caught his eye. Stiffly he crouched down and picked it up to inspect it. It was a child's baseball cap that looked like it had seen better days. It was worn and dirty, with some of the stitching coming loose at the edges. Something about it rang familiar to Father Fleming, but he couldn't place it. As he turned the cap over in his hands, examining it, he noticed something dried on the brim. Blood!

"Donovan Fleming," the wind whispered softly.

Hearing his name, Father Fleming jerked his head up and scanned the dimly lit church. "Whose there?" he called out.

"Salvation," the wind replied.

There was the soft rattle of chains somewhere to Father Fleming's left, drawing his attention. At first he saw nothing, then he spotted it. In the corner, beneath the huge wooden cross mounted on the wall, something moved in the shadows . . . Rather, the shadows themselves were moving.

"Demon," Father Fleming gasped, backing away.

The shadows chuckled. *"To some, yes. To others I am the word of the Lord. The* true *word of the Lord."*

Father Fleming crossed himself, and brandished the crucifix that dangled around his neck. "In the name of the Father, the Son and the—" His words were cut off when something whistled through the air, knocking the crucifix from his hand and opening up a gash on his cheek. His eyes landed on the culprit, a small metal cross with edges so sharp that it had embedded itself in the wood of the altar.

"The words only have power for those who believe, and you are no believer!" the voice accused. This time it sounded closer, almost directly behind him.

"For near thirty years I've been a faithful servant of the church and the people," Father Fleming shot back.

"Is that the script you read to gain the trust of the parents who left their children to your twisted devices? Did his parents believe you when you stood on your soapbox preaching false hope, while they grieved for their missing child?"

Father Fleming's eyes involuntarily shifted back to the baseball cap in his hand. He hadn't even realized he was still holding it. The pieces finally fell into place and he realized why the cap had been so familiar to him. The sight of the blood brought back memories Father Fleming thought long buried.

"I was sick back then," Father Fleming said, barely above a whisper. "I couldn't help myself. They were just so——"

"Tempting," the voice finished for him. *"The tender flesh . . . pretty pink, young lips. Children of soft and supple skin, smelling of dime-store candy and innocence."*

Something stirred low in Father Fleming and he felt warmth settling in the crotch of his pants as his penis rose ever so slightly. "No, no . . . That was before." He dropped to his knees in front of the altar. "The Lord has healed me and washed away my sins."

The voice laughed. There was a rush of air as a chain sprang from the darkness, tipped with a steel hook, and bit into Father Fleming's right forearm. Another followed it, this one hooking itself into the priest's left shoulder. The chains rattled as he was lifted to his feet like a puppet on strings. The pain was so intense that Father Fleming couldn't manage a scream, so he whimpered.

"Only blood can wash away sins," the voice spoke again. This time it was coming from directly in front of Father Fleming.

Through a haze of pain and tears he beheld his attacker. "Mother of God," he gasped, as cold, sharpened steel was suddenly placed against his throat.

"No, I am His justice."

Those were the last words Father Fleming heard before the blade released him from this world.

CHAPTER 1

FOR AS LONG AS ARCHIE JONES COULD REMEMBER, he always wanted to be a gangsta. As a kid he had been fascinated by crime. While other kids in his class aspired to be like LeBron James, Derek Jeter, or some other sports hero, Archie wanted to be like Scarface. Even when watching old *Batman* reruns with his siblings, he would be the one rooter for the Joker or some other archnemesis to finally take the hero down.

Eventually, Archie got his wish and was recruited by one of the local drug crews and officially initiated into a life of crime. It was a far less glamorous existence than Archie had anticipated, having to start from the bottom, but his prospects had started looking up recently. During a chance meeting through a friend, Archie had met a man looking to buy a large amount of cocaine. Archie didn't have any weight of his own to push, but he knew someone who did and brokered a meeting between the two. This brought him to a seedy diner on the outskirts of Queens in the wee hours of the night.

"Where the hell is your boy?" Smush asked, looking

down at his gold watch. They called him Smush because his nose laid flat on his face as if it had no cartilage. He was second in command of the crew Archie ran with, and the one sent to oversee this deal.

"I dunno, he was supposed to be here by now. Maybe he got stuck in traffic," Archie suggested.

"Well, I'm gonna give him five more minutes, then I'm leaving. I don't like my time being wasted."

"He'll be here," Archie assured Smush. The last thing he wanted was for the deal to fall through. Archie was not only looking forward to the broker's fee he'd been promised, but if the deal went well the boss would look favorably on him. It would be an opportunity for him to move another step up the ladder.

The doors to the diner swung open and in walked a man who seemed to immediately draw everyone's attention. He was tall, over six feet, and wide at the shoulders, with a Yankees fitted cap pulled low, shadowing his eyes. Long braids spilled from beneath the hat and tickled his shoulders. The black leather jacket he wore was shiny and slick with rain. One hand was shoved into the pocket of his jacket and in the other he held a briefcase. From beneath the brim of the cap, his dark eyes scanned the room. When he spotted Archie, he headed in his direction.

As he neared the table, two of Smush's boys rose to

meet him. They were mean-looking guys, both with gun butts jutting from their pants in plain sight. They stood between him and Smush, glaring.

The man peered up at them, allowing them to get a direct look at his face. He appeared youthful, clearly no older than his late twenties. He was a good-looking man, in a very rugged sort of way. With his shaggy sideburns, deeply cleft upper lip, and slightly pointed canine teeth, he bore a striking resemblance to a dog. "You gonna stand there gawking at me or ask me to dance?" he addressed the men blocking his path.

"Take it easy. That's my guy, Wolf. He's the one I was telling you about," Archie said excitedly. The men continued to stand there until Smush gave them the signal that it was okay to let him pass. One of the men moved but the other hesitated. He continued to stare at Wolf for a few more seconds before allowing him to pass.

"What's good, Archie?" Wolf removed his hand from his pocket and gave him dap.

"Waiting for you, so we can close this deal," Archie told him. "Wolf, this is Smush. Smush, this is Wolf."

"Good to meet you." Wolf extended his hand, but Smush made no move to shake it.

"So, I hear you're looking to buy some drugs?" Smush got right to the point.

"I hear you're looking to sell some drugs," Wolf

countered. "Now that both of our roles here are clearly defined, how about we get to it? I've got a few more moves to make after I leave here. You got what I need or what?"

Smush gave Archie a nod. Archie went into the bathroom and came out a few seconds later holding a paper bag, which he laid on the table in front of Wolf. The man peered inside the bag and saw a neatly wrapped bundle of cocaine.

"That there is the best shit in the city," Archie said proudly.

"I'll be the judge of that." Wolf pulled out a small pocketknife. "Do you mind?"

Smush shrugged, letting him know it was okay to test it. Wolf stuck the knife though the package and scooped a small amount of cocaine onto the blade. Holding it out for all to see, he then made the cocaine disappear up his nose. "Now that is some good shit," Wolf smiled after a moment as the cocaine hit him.

"I told you!" Archie said.

"Yeah, this is some good shit, but it looks a little light. I asked for three kilos, not one."

"I know what you asked for and that's what you'll get, after I see some bread," Smush told him.

"Right, the money," Wolf said, as if he was just re- membering he had to pay for it. "I got it for you right here." He placed the briefcase on the table and undid the locks before turning it to face Smush and motioning for him to do the honors.

Smush opened the case, expecting it to be filled with cash, but instead he found it empty, save for a silver badge that read, *NYPD*. The room got deathly silent. "What the fuck is this, some kind of joke?" Smush asked, looking from the badge to Wolf.

"No joke, my friend. You're under arrest. As a matter of fact, all of you drug-dealing shit bags are under arrest," Wolf said, motioning toward Smush's boys.

For a few seconds, Wolf and Smush simply glared at each other. Archie sat off to the side looking like he would break down into tears at any moment. He had brought Wolf to Smush and therefore would be held responsible for the colossal fuck-up.

"Fuck you, pig!" Smush then roared, and reached for the gun inside his jacket.

Wolf kicked the table, sending it sliding into Smush. When it collided with Smush's hand, the gun went off and a bullet nicked his side, before continuing to Archie's thigh where it pierced muscles and shattered his femur. Between Archie and Smush, it was hard to tell whose scream was the loudest. Wolf tried to reach for his own gun, but one of Smush's boys grabbed him from behind in a bear hug and yanked him from the chair.

"You know I'm going to have to add resisting arrest to your list of charges now, right?" Wolf said to the man holding him.

"Then it's a good thing you ain't gonna live long enough to file the report," the second man said, drawing his gun and aiming it at Wolf's face.

Just as he pulled the trigger, Wolf's legs shot up and kicked the gun, sending the bullet whistling past him and hitting an innocent bystander who had just entered the diner. Wolf threw his head back, breaking the nose of the man who had been holding him. When his grip slackened, Wolf fired both his elbows backward like torpedoes, connecting with the man's ribs and knocking the wind out of him. Wolf followed with a kick to the nuts, and when the man doubled over, he kneed him in the face and knocked him out of the fight.

The second man raised his arm to get off a second shot, but he was too close, which cost him dearly. Wolf grabbed the arm holding the gun and twisted until he heard the bone of his elbow snap. Without breaking his motion, Wolf drew his cuffs and secured the man to a chair by his injured arm.

"You boys see if you can sit tight and stay out of trouble while I finish my business with your boss," Wolf taunted his fallen opponents. When he turned to confront Smush, he found only Archie, who was whimpering as he struggled to his feet. He looked up and caught a glimpse of Smush disappearing through a door that said, *Employees Only.* "Stay down," Wolf ordered, before kicking Archie in the face and pursuing Smush.

Wolf drew his big .45 and pressed his back against the wall outside the doors he'd seen Smush leave through. It was hardly a police-regulation firearm, but Wolf had never been good with sticking with rules or regulations. After checking to make sure he was fully loaded, Wolf passed through the doors. He found himself in a storeroom, with rows of shelves stacked with boxes of liquor and glasses. Smush could've been hiding anywhere, so he moved cautiously. His eyes picked out what looked like drops of blood on the floor. When he bent down to examine them, a bullet shot past him and struck the shelf he had just been standing in front of. A stray piece of debris left a small cut across Wolf's cheek, trickling blood into his beard.

"You'll never take me alive!" Smush shouted from somewhere inside the room.

"Sounds good to me," Wolf replied, and went in search of his prey. His nose twitched, picking up the faint smell of nicotine, which he was sure marked Smush's passing. The shadows at the end of an aisle shifted a split second before Wolf saw a muzzle flash. He slid across the floor in time to avoid the bullets, and responded with three slugs of his own. He didn't hit his target, but he got Smush off his back long enough to scramble for proper cover, which he found behind a stack of crates near the fire exit. He could hear Smush shuffling around in the dark . . . wounded and afraid. The hunt was on.

Wolf spied movement on the other side of the boxes directly across from him. He could only see through the small creases between the boxes, so had it not been for the shift in the light he'd have never noticed Smush creeping. He was trying to come around the other side and get the drop on Wolf. If it was a drop he wanted, then a drop he would get.

Smush's side was on fire. He was losing blood and feared that he would pass out at any moment, but the threat of going to prison for a very long time kept him conscious. He had fucked himself by trying to do side business with Archie, after his boss had already told him not to. Smush had secretly gone forward with the deal out of greed and the need to prove that he could make his own moves, and now it was costing him.

He heard something shifting above his head and glanced up to the top tier of the shelf just in time to see something speeding his way. He barely had time to raise his arms in defense before the heavy wooden box landed on him. He knew without seeing a doctor that both of his arms were broken and he probably had a concussion. Smush wanted to just lay there and die, but the pain of someone pulling at one of his broken arms wouldn't let him slip away.

"As I was saying earlier," Wolf began, while putting his spare handcuffs on Smush's wrists, "your drug-selling ass is under arrest."

By the time Wolf had brought his quarry out of the storeroom, the diner was filled with police. Archie and the two goons were being led out, and from the bathroom two uniformed officers appeared holding the remaining cocaine. Wolf couldn't believe they'd been dumb enough to have it all stashed in one spot. It was a victory for the department and everyone was smiling, except Wolf's superior officer, Detective Sergeant Grady.

Sergeant Tasha Grady was the subject of many whispers in the department, in and out of the locker room. She was a brown-skinned woman in her late thirties, yet with the body of a twenty-five-year-old that she didn't mind showing off. Before joining the force she'd had a budding career as a model, but she gave it up to put her life on the line every night for the city she had been born and raised in. Being eye candy *and* an African American woman, Grady had to work twice as hard as anyone else to earn respect on the force, though she was more than up to the challenge. She'd started out as a uniformed beat walker on the streets of Harlem and had climbed the ladder quickly, due in part to her network of confidential informants and snitches. Grady had eyes and ears everywhere, but would never reveal the identities of the people who fed her information. None could say for sure why she guarded the list so closely, yet there was speculation. One rumor linked her romantically to a suspected assassin who went by the name Animal. Rumors and speculation aside, no one could deny that Grady was an efficient cop.

Grady stood there, in the middle of the mess Wolf had made, wearing a tight-fitting gray skirt with a matching blazer. Her tall black heels were resting in a pool of blood, though she didn't seem to notice. Her face was often inviting and warm, but not at that moment. Grady looked like she was about to blow a gasket. Wolf handed Smush off to one of the uniformed officers to be booked and went to take his medicine.

"Wherever there's a mess, there's Lone Wolf James," Grady addressed him by the moniker he'd earned during his years on the force for his solo tactics.

"Good evening, Detective Sergeant Grady," Wolf said pleasantly.

"What's so good about it? I'm in a shithole diner in the middle of the night, it's raining, they're loading a premed student who got hit by a stray bullet into an ambulance, this is going to require tons of paperwork, and I'm left to clean it all up because my lieutenant had a brunch appointment with his mistress that demanded his immediate attention. So tell me again what's so good about this evening?" Grady replied.

"Listen, Grady, I can explain—"

"Save it," she waved him silent. "I got the short version on the way over here. The plan was for you to come in and negotiate the deal while tactical teams moved into place, then leave and let them do the rest, not go John Rambo and shoot up the damn place! Jesus, Wolf, sometimes I think you're *trying* to get yourself kicked off the force."

"All I'm trying to do is good police work," Wolf told her.

"Since when did making things up as you go along become good police work? It was a simple buy-and-bust and you turned it into a shoot-out," Grady scolded him. "And speaking of buy, where's the buy money? They said the briefcase was empty."

"The buy money is in the car. What, did you think I stole it?" Wolf asked sarcastically.

"That's not what I meant, Wolf. It's just that everything has to be accounted for or it falls on me."

"Whatever you say, sergeant. The money is in the

car. You're more than welcome to count it to make sure I didn't pinch anything off the top."

"I don't think that'll be necessary. Wolf, I know you think I'm busting your balls, but I'm just trying to look out for you. With the rash of reckless police activity against the public, they're really cracking down trying to save face. You can't keep at this lone-wolf thing."

"Look, the important thing is we accomplished our goal by taking another scumbag and his drugs off the streets. That was the game plan and I got it done; I don't see what the big deal is about *how* I got it done."

"The big deal is that you not only put your team in jeopardy by jumping the gun, you put civilians at risk!" Grady said heatedly. "How much of this cowboy shit do you think those people downtown are gonna take before they bury you in a hole somewhere and hand your mama a folded flag along with their condolences?"

"They can do what they like, but it isn't gonna change how I do my job. If I have to knock a few heads to get it done, then heads will be knocked. This is the fucking jungle, not the golf course. They're playing for keeps and so am I. When the brass decides they wanna climb from behind those nice desks and get out here in the trenches, then they can tell me how to work these streets."

"James," Grady called him now by his first name, "I

come from the same thing you come from, so don't try it with me. You've already dodged one bullet by the skin of your teeth and the next fuck-up is likely to have you out on your ass or brought up on charges. I know how hard it is trying to make a difference out here, but pissing on the rules isn't going to help."

"I'm not pissing on the rules, I'm just rewriting them," Wolf said smugly.

Grady was about to respond when a uniformed officer walked up and whispered something in her ear. A sour expression crossed her face. "What do they want with him?" she asked, not hiding the fact that she was annoyed.

"I don't know, ma'am. I was just told to relay the message," the officer answered before leaving.

"Everything okay?" Wolf asked.

"Why don't *you* tell me? Your presence has just been requested at the scene of a homicide."

Wolf scoffed. "I don't answer to homicide, I'm narcotics. So tell whatever lieutenant is requesting me that I don't get sent for like some lackey."

"It wasn't a lieutenant who sent for you. This summons came from Captain Marx directly."

CHAPTER 2

I T WAS JUST BEFORE DAWN WHEN THE CALL CAME IN. A basehead look-ing for a discrete spot to blast off had crept in through an open back door of the building and discovered the body. He called it in to the police, hoping to get a reward to put toward his next high, but all he got was detained for questioning. A wall of uniformed officers ringed the perimeter, keeping everyone at a safe distance so as not to contaminate the crime scene. Since word got out, the block had turned into a circus of media and concerned citizens wondering about the heavy police presence in the normally quiet neighborhood.

The black-on-black Escalade drew more than a few curious stares when it rolled to a stop at the curb, twenty-two-inch chrome rims twinkling in the morn-ing sun. 2Pac's "All Eyez on Me" poured through the sound system when the car door swung open and Detec-tive Wolf oozed from behind the wheel. He'd made a pit stop along the way over to change out of the clothes he'd been wearing at the bust and was now dressed in a black sweatsuit with a black bandanna tied around his head.

His whole aura screamed thug, and the crowd gave him a wide berth as he approached the crime scene.

A ruddy-faced youth in a baggy blue uniform, who had obviously seen one too many reruns of *NYPD Blue*, moved to cut Wolf off. His face was sour and his hand lingered near his gun when he spoke. "Move it along, *homie*. They ain't giving away no free turkeys today, this is police business."

Wolf took a long drag off his cigarette and let the smoke spill from his nostrils. "I see you got jokes," he laughed. "Stand aside before you find yourself disciplined for trying to be a comedian." He reached to lift the police tape, so he could duck under and enter the crime scene, but the officer grabbed him about the wrist. Wolf's eyes traveled up from the officer's hand to his face. His lips drew back into a sneer, making him look every bit of the animal he was named after. "I'll give you until the count of three before I put you on the news." His hands balled into two tight fists.

"You threatening me?" The officer now gripped his weapon, his other hand still holding Wolf's wrist.

"One . . ."

Another blue shirt approached. "What's going on over here?"

"Two . . ."

"Stand down, officers," a gruff voice called out

before Wolf could finish his count. A pale man, who looked like he hadn't been getting enough sun, emerged from the church doorway. A thick salt-and-pepper beard almost completely hid his upper lip. The captain's bars on his white shirt glistened in the sun as if they were made of real gold.

At the sight of the captain the young officer released Wolf's arm and took a step back. Both he and the second officer stood straight as boards, trying to look the part of model law enforcement in the presence of their superior.

"What the hell are you doing?" Captain Marx asked.

"We were just trying to keep the crime scene clear of rabble-rousers like you asked, sir," the ruddy-face officer spoke up.

"You've got one more chance to call me by anything other than my name and I'm gonna put your lights out," Wolf warned the young officer.

"You raise your hand in the presence of your captain and I'll make sure you spend the next six months sucking fumes at the Holland Tunnel while you're directing rush hour traffic, detective!" Captain Marx snapped.

"*Detective?*" the two uniformed officers said in unison.

Wolf pulled out the gold rope chain from inside his sweat jacket and flashed the badge hanging from the end of it. "Detective James Wolf."

"Lone Wolf James," the second officer spat, as if the words tasted like ash in his mouth. James Wolf had quite the reputation amongst his peers and superiors.

"My friends call me Wolf, and we ain't friends, so Detective Wolf is fine. Now get the fuck out of my way so I can do my job." He ducked under the tape and brushed past the two officers.

"Must you make a grand entrance every time you go somewhere, Jimmy?" Captain Marx asked, leading him up the church steps.

"I prefer Wolf or James, if you must. And I get my grand old entrances from my daddy," he said with an easy smile. His father, James "Jimmy" Wolf Sr., had been a blues singer in the late '70s and early '80s. He loved to sing, but he loved cocaine more, and it was his first love that put him in an early grave and left James Jr. and his mother alone and struggling. "So, what's so important that a police captain calls on a wretch like me at the crack of dawn?"

"Don't get cute with me, Wolf. Under these bars and this white shirt I'm still the same guy who used to knock your skinny ass around the ring when I was training you," Captain Marx reminded him. Many years prior, Wolf was one of the young kids who had joined the boxing program at the Police Athletic League where Marx volunteered as a trainer. Back then Wolf was barely one hundred pounds, but he was faster than any man Marx had ever seen. He could've been a great fighter, but didn't have the discipline to focus more on boxing than the streets.

"I hit a lot harder now than I did when I was fourteen," Wolf told him.

"I guess one of these weekends we can climb back in the ring and see what you've learned, but that'll have to wait. Right now, let's focus on police business."

"What's going on, cap?" Wolf asked, suddenly feeling uneasy about the look on Marx's face. Clearly, whatever he had brought Wolf there to see had him troubled, and it took a lot to trouble a man like Captain Marx.

The captain didn't bother to answer. Instead, he turned on his heels and walked inside the church. Wolf stood there for a few moments, staring up at the stonework of the church. Standing in the massive building's shadow made him uneasy. His gut began churning. It was as if his feet simply touching the steps of the church soiled them . . . made them unclean, like him, and with every step he took toward the arched entrance, the corruption spread.

When Wolf crossed the threshold of the church, the first thing he noticed was the smell. It was a combination of mothballs and death. He ignored the detectives and uniformed officers whose eyes followed him as he trailed

Captain Marx into the chapel. Once there, it only took a second for him to spot it. Every other eye in the room was turned to it too. There was a series of flashes as a medical examiner snapped pictures of the crime scene from different angles. Suspended above the altar of the church was obviously what had Captain Marx so rattled.

The victim was a Caucasian man who looked to be somewhere in his late fifties, though it was hard to tell for sure considering his condition. He was suspended from the ceiling by chains, like a side of beef in a butcher's freezer. Wolf could see where the steel hooks snaked beneath his skin, stretching it so much in some spots that it looked like it was about to tear away from his body. The blood-soaked white collar around his neck said that he was a priest, or at least he had been before someone strung him up. Now he was just meat dripping onto the wood floor.

"Nasty piece of work, isn't it?" Captain Marx said.

"More like sick! Who would carve up a priest like that?" Wolf asked.

"That's what we're trying to figure out. Father Fleming was a good man. No enemies to speak of."

"You mean no enemies that you *know* of. Nobody gets dusted for nothing, especially not a priest. What kind of fucked-up individual would do something like this?"

"I was hoping that you could tell me."

"Me?" For the last few years Wolf had been working in narcotics. Homicide wasn't his bag.

Before the Captain Marx could clue him in, they were interrupted by two approaching men. The first was dark-skinned, with a tapered Afro and wearing a wrinkled green suit. The second was a tall Latino man dressed in jeans and a long-sleeved white shirt. Gold badges were visible on both of them.

"What's he doing here? This isn't a drug case," Detective Brown, the one with the Afro, said.

"Blood always brings the wolves out," Wolf responded, just to get under the detective's skin. There was no love lost between the two.

"Well, no pets are allowed in here, so why don't you let your master take you for a walk, dog," the second man, Detective Alvarez, said before crossing his heavily tattooed arms.

Wolf's brow furrowed. He was being tested. "If you're trying to be funny, I got a joke that I wanna share too, only you have to step outside for me to tell it."

"What're you gonna do, shoot us and try to put it down on the books as righteous, like you did your last partner?" Detective Brown said scornfully. It was a low blow and he knew it.

Before Wolf realized what he was doing, he lunged

for Detective Brown. The two detectives began tussling, with Wolf wrapping his hands around Brown's neck, trying to choke the breath from his body.

"Enough!" Captain Marx tried to pull the men apart, but they were locked onto each other like pit bulls. It took the combined efforts of Marx and Alvarez to separate them.

"Smile, officers!" someone called out. When they turned around, a photographer who had slipped into the church began snapping pictures.

"Who let him in here? Get that son of a bitch out of here and confiscate that damn camera!" Captain Marx raged. Two uniformed officers grabbed the photographer and dragged him from the church. "Have the both of you lost your fucking minds?" He looked back and forth between the two scrapping detectives.

"Your boy has got a smart fucking mouth," Wolf said, staring daggers at Detective Brown.

"Then why don't you come and close it for me?" Brown challenged.

Wolf took a step in his direction, but Captain Marx blocked his path. "Don't push your luck with me, Jimmy. I'm still your boss."

"James," Wolf grumbled.

Captain Marx ignored him and turned to Detective Brown. "Why don't you take a walk and cool off."

"You can't be serious," Detective Brown said.

"Captain, with all due respect, this is *our* crime scene," Detective Alvarez declared.

"And it'll still be *your* crime scene when you get back," Captain Marx replied.

Detective Alvarez wanted to argue, but he knew it would be pointless: Marx outranked him. "Come on, you know we ain't got no wins when it comes to the captain's pet dog." He patted Detective Brown on the chest, and led him to the door.

Detective Brown was so angry that you could almost see steam rising from his head. Before he left the chapel, he stopped short and stared at Wolf. "One of these days the captain isn't going to be around to save your ass. If you're not careful, you might find yourself the victim of friendly fire, just like Dutton." He winked at Wolf and left the room.

"Are you intentionally trying to get yourself kicked off the force?" Captain Marx asked Wolf once the other two detectives were gone.

"Hey, if I have to lose my job because I won't let assholes like Brown disrespect me, then so be it."

"So what, you gonna sock everybody in the chin who says something hurtful to you? If that's the case, you're gonna have a whole lot of fighting to do."

Wolf snorted. "I been fighting all my life, that ain't

nothing new. You of all people should know that."

"Yeah, kid. You're a fighter, and I've seen you put quite a few people on their asses, but there's one you've never been able to beat."

"Bullshit, I never lost a fight in the ring!" Wolf countered.

Captain Marx placed his hand on Wolf's shoulder. "I'm not talking about the ring, kid, I'm talking about that ghost you keep swinging at and can't seem to hit. When are you gonna let it go?"

Wolf wished it was that simple. He wished he could put what he was feeling in the bottom of a file cabinet with the official report, that he could wash away the evils of the job in booze like most cops did, but blood didn't wash off him so easily. "I know you didn't call me here to discuss my service record. What gives, captain?" he asked, ignoring the question.

"I was hoping you could help give me some insight into what we're dealing with." Captain Marx nodded toward the dead body. "At a glance, how would you call it?"

Wolf walked to the edge of the police tape and examined the body. "The blood splatter patterns are what I would look at first," Wolf began. "You see the way the ones around the body are drying already and the ones pooling under the body are still wet? They're older, and from the way they're spraying away from the body," he pointed to the faint splotches of blood just beyond the police tape, "I'd say he was hung on the chains while he was still alive. His throat was cut later. The killer wanted him to suffer, which means it was personal and not some random killing."

Captain Marx nodded. "Very good. It's nice to know that there's still a cop hiding somewhere beneath that chip you're carrying around on your shoulder."

"Okay, so somebody whacked a priest, my heart is bleeding. I still don't see what it has to do with me. Like your boys said, I'm narcotics and they're homicide. Let those two idiots work the case."

"They *are* going to work the case, but I need you to *solve* it. And the quicker the better," Captain Marx said with a nervous edge to his voice.

Wolf picked up on his superior's uneasiness. "Captain, what is it about this murder that you aren't telling me?"

"I fear that the chickens may be coming home to roost," Captain Marx answered in a defeated tone. Before explaining further, he led Wolf to a quiet corner away from the crime scene. He spared a glance over his shoulder before reaching into his pocket and producing a plastic baggie, which he discretely passed to Wolf.

Wolf examined the strange flower inside. It looked

almost like a water lily, only it was as black as night. "What is it?"

"Temporarily misplaced evidence," Captain Marx said with a sly grin. "It's a *Nelumbo lutea*, also known as the American lotus."

"I've seen lotuses before, but never a black one." Wolf handed the flower back to Captain Marx.

"I have, and I've prayed that I'd never see one again. I've only seen one up close once in my life before this, and it was at the scene of a multiple homicide, even more fucked up than this one. We were looking for a little girl who had been kidnapped by a Mexican cartel. Thanks to an anonymous tip we were able to track them to a warehouse out near the airport. Now keep in mind that these were highly trained and ruthless killers, so when we go in we're already expecting the worst, but none of us expected what we encountered when we got inside."

"Did it get messy?"

Captain Marx laughed. "That's just it. We were able to put it to bed without firing a single shot, thanks to that little black flower."

"I don't understand."

"Neither did we. When we rushed the warehouse, instead of finding the dozen or so shooters we'd pre-pared for, we found a warehouse full of corpses. There were eight or nine of them all together, all gutted and hung from the ceiling by chains like cattle. Same as Father Fleming."

"And the girl?" Wolf asked.

"Physically, she was fine except for the fact that she was covered in blood. Mentally, she was stir-fried. It was days before we could get her to do anything besides mumble incoherently in Spanish. When we were finally able to question her, she had quite a story to tell. She said that the Angel of Death had come and killed the men."

"So you mean to say that one person came in and took out a room full of armed cartel gunmen?"

"Sounded like a tall tale to me too, until I asked her to describe the Angel of Death, and all she would say was, *El Loto Negro.*"

"The Black Lotus," Wolf translated, drawing on his high school Spanish skills. Something about the name sounded familiar, but he wasn't sure why.

"Right," Captain Marx nodded. "I did some digging and found a few other cases that mentioned a black flower at the scene of the crime. Just about all the victims had been criminals of some sort, or had some black mark on their record. The causes of death were different, but there was a flower at every scene."

"So, you think we're dealing with some type of serial killer?" Wolf was growing more interested. He hadn't officially agreed to help with the case yet, but his brain was processing the information as if he had.

Captain Marx chuckled. "A serial killer would've made this too easy. I believe this is way bigger. During my investigation into the Black Lotus I kept getting stonewalled by the department, so I called a buddy of mine who works for the feds. From the way he reacted you'd think I'd just asked him to help me whack the president. Officially, he refused to comment on the Black Lotus killings."

"But unofficially?"

"Unofficially, he told me that the Black Lotus is an assassin rumored to be tied to the BHOB. You might know them as the Brotherhood of Blood."

This surprised Wolf. He didn't have any official information on the Brotherhood, but from what he'd heard they were a secret fraternity of assassins, who were hailed as the best of the best when it came to taking lives. The Brotherhood of Blood was alleged to be connected to some of the most infamous killings in American history, but they moved like ghosts, so law enforcement was never able to put anything other than speculation on paper about them. Their members were said to be composed of men from all walks of life, and none outside of the Brotherhood knew the true identities of its members.

"I've always thought tales of the Brotherhood were ghost stories to keep rookies on their toes," Wolf said.

"Ghost stories don't leave priests strung up like meat in a slaughterhouse." Captain Marx glanced over at the murdered man.

Wolf turned his gaze as well to the mess that had been Father Fleming. He reassessed the crime scene, the chains, the worn wooden benches . . . the red baseball cap lying on the floor . . . He hadn't noticed that cap at first because it was soaked in blood, and almost blended in with the bloody floor. Something about it tugged at his brain, but before he could dwell on it further, the captain broke his concentration.

"So, are you with me or what?"

Wolf weighed it. "Let's say I go along with the theory that the priest was killed by someone from the Brotherhood. What does it have to do with me? It isn't drug related, so why should I get involved? You said yourself that the department was stonewalling you and the feds don't wanna talk about it, so why not just leave it alone? Or better yet, let those two idiots from homicide deal with it. I'm sure the department will be more inclined to lend their support to the donkeys than they would the wolf." He didn't bother to hide the sarcasm in his voice.

"If I go to my superiors talking about secret societies and assassins, they're likely to slap me in a white coat and lock me away somewhere. Brown and Alvarez are good cops, and given enough time I'm sure they'll piece it together, but by then the shit will already have hit the fan and the Brotherhood will be in the wind. Once they're called in to do a job, they don't waste much time."

"For someone who doesn't know much about the Brotherhood, you seem pretty well informed as to their tactics," Wolf said. It was more of an observation than an accusation, but it somehow felt like the latter.

Captain Marx shrugged. "You're in the streets so you know how it goes. Sometimes you hear things. Listen, James, you know I wouldn't come to you unless it was a last resort. I need someone I can trust to help me out on this one. I'm not asking as your captain, I'm asking as your friend."

Wolf took a few minutes to mull over what Captain Marx was asking him. It would be a difficult case, with him having very little to go on, and obviously dangerous, but those were the elements that got Wolf out of bed every morning to put on his badge. "This could get very messy, captain," he finally said.

"I'm sure it will, but I'll make it worth your while. You crack this case and I'll make all that Dutton business go away."

Detective Richie Dutton had at one time been Wolf's partner and mentor. They called him the Chameleon

because of how fluidly he slipped from one criminal per-
sona to the next. He was so good that sometimes it was
hard to tell which side of the law he was really on. He
taught Wolf how to survive working undercover cases
by embracing the personas of the criminals they were
tracking. When Wolf and Dutton were on the job they
moved like rock stars, indulging in money, pussy, and
drugs—and it was the drugs that eventually tore them
apart.

Wolf dabbled in drugs when the job called for it,
but Richie was over-the-top with it. He was notorious
for his cocaine and alcohol binges. One night he had
gotten coked up out of his mind and beat a prostitute
they'd had working as a CI nearly to death. When she
threatened to blow his cover, Richie decided that she
had to go. Wolf had done some things that he wasn't
proud of while working undercover, but he wouldn't sign
off on cold-blooded murder. The two got into a heated
argument over it and one thing led to another. When
it was all said and done, Dutton and the CI ended up
dead and Wolf was left to answer for the killings. In his
report he said that Dutton had been high on drugs and
trying to kill him, so he'd shot his partner in self-defense.
The toxicology report confirmed that Detective Dutton
had elevated levels of cocaine, marijuana, and alcohol
in his system, and being that there were no witnesses, no

charges were brought against Wolf. The shooting was ruled justified, though there were still some people who weren't convinced.

"I was cleared of that," Wolf replied.

"Yeah, for now. You think I don't know that IAD is still sniffing around, trying to find a home for that dirty kill?"

"They can sniff all they want, but they won't find anything," Wolf replied confidently.

"Yeah, because it was me who taught you how to cover your tracks. Look, whether it went down the way you say it did or not isn't my call to make. I'm not judging, but as long as you have that hovering over your head, your service record is going to always be tainted. I'm offering to wipe your slate clean. You might even be able to pull a promotion out of it if you solve the case."

"And if I blow it?"

"If you blow it, some heads are going to roll, starting with yours. I'll deny any knowledge of your investigation, but will do what I can to see that you're not brought up on charges," Captain Marx said flatly.

Wolf couldn't help but laugh. "You're one cold old bastard."

"The least I can do is be honest with you. It's no secret that with all the complaints filed against you, you're one dumb-ass decision away from going to state prison.

You need this break as much as I do. So what do you say? Can I count on you?"

"If I do this, captain, I do it my way."

"I wouldn't have it any other way. With this case, the rules go out the window. This is your baby to put to bed," Captain Marx agreed.

"Fair enough. Do you at least have a starting point for me?" Wolf asked.

Captain Marx pulled a sheet of paper from his pocket and handed it to him. "I'd say pay them a visit first. They're members of the late Father Flemming's congregation and amongst the last people to see him alive."

"I'm on it," Wolf said, slipping the paper into his pocket.

"Remember, Wolf, I need you to be discrete. Try not to kill anyone or destroy any property, okay?"

"I'm not making any promises, but I'll do my best." Wolf gave him a wink and started for the chapel door. On his way out he had some last words for Marx: "And just to give you fair warning, if your boys Brown and Alvarez get in my way, I can't be held accountable for what happens to them."

Long after Detective Wolf had gone, Captain Marx continued staring at the exit. A part of him felt bad about sending Wolf off half-cocked, but he was desperate. He knew more about the Black Lotus killer than he'd let on, but to admit this would mean opening up a can of worms that he wasn't ready to address. If he didn't get the situation under control there would be a shit storm that would surely rain on his head. Being fired and losing his pension were the least of his concerns, though. He was more worried about someone finding him hanging from a ceiling like Father Fleming.

Wolf jumped back in his truck and fired up the engine. He had a lot to do and not a lot of time, so he would get started immediately. He would visit the people Captain Marx had suggested and work from there. When he pulled the sheet of paper from his pocket to put the address in his GPS, he realized that he knew the location. His last visit to the address was the reason he had transferred out of missing persons and joined the narcotics task force.

CHAPTER 3

KAHLLAH SAT AT HER DESK, HUNCHED OVER A COPY of the latest issue of the *Village Voice*. She chewed the tip of her highlighter, as she often did when she was deep in thought, scanning through the pages like she was looking for a needle in a haystack. She had been up half the night trying to catch up on a backlog of editorial work, and was in dire need of a nap, but there was too much to do. Sleep would have to wait. When the letters started dancing on the page in front of her, she knew it was time to take a break.

She stood up and stretched her five-nine frame, trying to get rid of the stiffness in her back, and flinched when she felt the soreness in her arms. "I need to cut back on the training," she said to no one in particular.

Kahllah walked over and stared out her office window. She could see the park a few blocks away and New Jersey just across the water. When they'd purchased the dilapidated brownstone to build what would be their first official office, she knew she had to have that room, just for the view. Kahllah had even had the contractors

knock out the wall and make it one big window. She
would sometimes stand there for hours watching the city
and the people in it. It filled her heart with pride when
she reflected on how two college kids with a crazy idea
had managed to build the foundation of something special.

Real Talk had started out as an online blog created
by Kahllah and her roommate Audrey back in college.
They'd noticed that there was a void of material that
appealed to young women their age besides gossip sites
and rap music blogs, so they decided to try and fill it. In
the beginning they mostly wrote about stuff like how to
navigate your way through college on a budget, the qual-
ity of food in the cafeteria, and the importance of keeping the toilet seat down in the coed bathrooms, but as
their audience expanded, so did their content. *Real Talk*
began to address more serious issues like the misman-
agement of the school's budget, diverting more money
into athletics than any other program including campus
safety. It was Kahllah and Audrey who forced the school
to call in the state police when campus security botched
the case of a girl who had been raped a few months
prior. Though the assailant was never caught, the ges-
ture pushed *Real Talk* into the spotlight. After graduation
Audrey pursued a career in journalism, while Kahllah
travelled the country with her father. A few years later
when the girls reconnected, Kahllah was able to finance

their dream of turning *Real Talk* into more than just a blog and Audrey was able to quit her day job. Audrey never asked where Kahllah got the money, and Kahllah never offered to tell her. Kahllah and Audrey were more like sisters than friends, but she wasn't sure Audrey would be able to handle the truth about what she had really been doing during their years apart. She hadn't lied when she said she'd been continuing her education, but the things she been studying weren't taught in any classroom. It was best to leave that part of her life buried and enjoy seeing their dream finally come to fruition.

Kahllah ran her hands through her jet-black hair and began massaging her scalp. Her fingers got a little tangled at the roots and she tried to remember the last time she had treated herself to a trip to the beauty parlor. Kahllah rarely went through the hassle of primping, or bothering with makeup. A little lip liner and a ponytail and she was good to go. Though she didn't put much stock in physical appearance, you couldn't deny she was a beautiful girl. She had bronze-colored skin and eyes that danced between butterscotch and deep brown, depending on her mood. It was nearly impossible to guess her ethnicity, though she got a kick out of watching people try. Some people mistook her for Dominican, while others thought maybe she was of Arab decent. Neither was correct. Kahllah was born in a small village outside East Kalimantan, Indonesia, to a dirt-poor family. Her mother was a native, and her father a black man from the United States doing charity work overseas. Cancer took her mother when Kahllah was six and a burglar took her father when she was nine. For the next few years she wandered the countryside, stealing when she could and starving when she couldn't. She eventually found herself a captive of a group of slave traders, who special-ized in child prostitution. The things they did to Kahllah they called "conditioning," but rape by any other name was still rape. When they were done abusing her, and al-lowing others to sample her sweet young flesh for a few coins, she was sold to a rich man in Africa. She thought this man might be her salvation, but he turned out to be worse than the slave traders. The African subjected Kahllah to all forms of mental and physical torture, and just about every night she spent with him she wished for death to free her from the living hell. Her wish wouldn't be granted until years later, but it was the African who death came for, not her. He was murdered in front of her over a debt owed, by a masked assassin. Kahllah expected to join her master in hell, but for reasons that were unclear to her at the time, the assassin spared her. She spent a short time in what was essentially a foster care system before she was adopted by an important man from America, who had the money and connections to bypass all the legal red tape. Her adopted father was a hard man and a war veteran, but he wasn't cruel. Before long, he whisked Kahllah away to the United States where the orphan girl was given a fresh start, a top-notch education, and a purpose.

Since obtaining her freedom, Kahllah had devoted a good portion of her life and her income to helping young women who were in dire situations. Though she had made it out, there were thousands of young girls across the globe who never would, unless someone took a stand. Kahllah was determined to do whatever she could to see that no woman was ever subjected to the same horrors she had faced while growing up.

Kahllah turned when she heard the office door suddenly open. Audrey walked in, balancing a cup of coffee and a doughnut in one hand and a newspaper in the other. Audrey was pretty girl who leaned toward chubby, but still had a nice shape and a style all her own. She was wearing a pair of black leggings and lime-green shoes, with a purple leather jacket that looked stolen from a Prince video shoot. At five four, Audrey was a woman who was short in height but big in personality. She was so engrossed in whatever she was reading that she didn't even notice Kahllah standing there.

"I guess knocking has become a lost art," Kahllah announced, jolting Audrey out of her newspaper article.

"You scared the hell out of me!" Audrey gasped. "What are you doing skulking around here like that?" She placed her wide ass on Kahllah's desk, inadvertently shoving the laptop aside.

"The last time I checked, it was still my office." Kahllah picked up the coffee cup Audrey had just set down and sipped from it. She frowned at the bitter taste. "How can you drink this shit?" She handed it back.

"I need something to keep me up and moving while I'm running the company and you're jet-setting. Where were you this time? Dubai? Paris?"

"Actually, Queens." Kahllah slid her a white folder with the name *Margaret Stone* written on it in red marker. Margaret Stone was a well-known advocate for women's rights and wife of a high-profile district attorney. Some called her a Joan of Arc for the modern era. "She's just cut the ribbon on a new women's shelter her organization helped build and I was doing a piece on it, so it was work related."

Audrey ignored the folder. "It's always work related when you disappear without a trace. One day I'm going to have to tag along on one of these excursions."

"Audrey, you and I both know you wouldn't last five minutes on the streets. I do the dirty work and you're the cute face of the company. That's always been our arrangement."

Audrey rolled her eyes. "You make it sound like I don't pull my weight around here. I do my part digging up stories."

"I agree, but most of your stories come from motel rooms and seedy bars," Kahllah joked.

"Fuck you, Kahllah," Audrey laughed. "Just because I'd rather have a good time than stalk back alleys doesn't mean my work is less important than yours."

"Whatever you say, Audrey." Kahllah winked play-fully. "Have you seen Roger today?"

"I sent him out on some deliveries. With any luck, he'll be gone all day. That guy gives me the creeps and I hate it when he's around the office and you're not here. He just sits in the corner doing those damn crossword puzzles and stares at people."

"Roger is harmless, he just needs constant direction. That's all," Kahllah said.

"Then I wish you would direct him someplace else to work. Me and some of the other girls were talking and we don't know how comfortable we feel working around that retard." The minute the word left Audrey's mouth, she wished she could take it back. Everyone in the office knew how Kahllah felt about Roger, and to speak ill of him was to bring Kahllah's wrath down on your head.

Roger was a veteran who hadn't come back from the war in one piece. He'd miraculously survived a slug to the head, but suffered brain damage as a result. Kahllah had found him living on the streets and selling crack for the local dealers, who paid him in food instead of cash. Because of her adopted father, Kahllah had always had a soft spot for US veterans and offered the young man a job at *Real Talk*, doing odd jobs and making deliveries. Unfortunately, the crack dealers he was working for were reluctant to let him go, so it took a bit of convincing. There were different variations of the story as to how Kahllah had gained Roger his freedom. Some said she'd bought his freedom from the dealers, while others said she called in a favor from a friend in the police department. The least talked about version, and probably the closest to the truth, ended with Kahllah's dad putting two of the dealers in the hospital. She would never confirm or deny any of the stories. Since then she had been looking out for Roger like a big sister.

"You need to watch your mouth, Audrey," Kahllah hissed.

"I'm sorry, K. You know I didn't mean any harm."

"I can't tell." Kahllah placed her palms on the table and gave Audrey a stern look. "Listen, I know Roger is a bit different and can sometimes be a lot to deal with, but he's still a person and has every right to earn a living.

This is the last time I plan on telling you or anyone else in this office that. Are we clear?"

"Sure thing, boss," Audrey said in her best Southern drawl.

"Don't be a smartass, Audrey, just try and be mindful of other people's feelings. I've got enough work to do without having to tell everyone in the office to stop teasing the slow kid."

"All you ever do is work, Kahllah. What are you reading up on?" Audrey snatched up the *Village Voice* from the desk before Kahllah could stop her. "The classifieds? Kahllah, I know you're not *that* hard up for a date."

"Give it back." Kahllah reached for the paper, but Audrey scooted out of her reach.

"*Older man working in transportation services seeks company of younger woman for rough play.* Signed, *Must Love Flowers*," Audrey read from one of the ads Kahllah had circled. "This is not only dangerous, it's depressing. As fine as you are, there's no way in the hell you should be scraping the bottom of the barrel for a date. Hell, I've got a cousin who'll be out of prison in a few months that I could introduce you to if you're this desperate."

"I have no interest in meeting your jailbird-ass cousin, and no, I'm not that hard up for a date." Kahllah snatched the paper from her. "I'm doing research for a story."

"Umm-hmm," Audrey gave her the side-eye. "Kahllah, you were always kind of stiff, but you were way more fun in college. I even recall you going out on a few dates, but when you came back to New York you were like a robot. I don't recall seeing you date anyone or so much as hearing you talk about a guy in months."

"I date here and there, Audrey, but I work too much to date anyone steadily. You see the kind of hours I keep. Our numbers at *Real Talk* are good, but they could be better. For them to get better, we have to find better stories. That's part of the reason I'm always traveling."

"Well, while you're off traveling, some of the best stories are going on right under our noses." Audrey tossed the newspaper that she'd been reading onto her friend's desk.

Kahllah's eyes widened in shock when she saw the headline about a priest who had been found murdered in his church. As she read the article that chronicled the man's service in the community over the past twenty years, up to his brutal murder by an unknown assailant, she found herself disgusted. "There are some sick people in the world. It's news, but these aren't the kind of stories *Real Talk* is about."

"Not what happened to the priest, the accompanying story at the bottom." Audrey tapped her finger on a smaller article that Kahllah had missed. It was a short piece about two detectives who had gotten into a fistfight at the scene of the crime. One of the detectives was listed as James Wolf, who had been one of the recent subjects of an investigation into police corruption. Above the story there was a grainy picture of a man dressed like a thug choking another man wearing a suit.

Kahllah shook her head. "Those fools at the NYPD are worse than reality TV."

"And these are the kind of stories that younger and hipper readers want! They want to read about people like Detective Wolf."

Kahllah shrugged. "One dirty cop is just as rotten as the next. I don't see what's so special about him."

"Then allow me to enlighten you. When I caught wind of this, I did a little digging and found that this cop is so dirty that his middle name should be Mud. His jacket reads like an episode of *Miami Vice*. He's been written up three times in the past eighteen months for misconduct and questioned twice about missing evidence in some of his cases. Two years ago he was even charged with murder."

This got Kahllah's attention. "Then what's he doing still wearing a badge?"

"Nobody would come forward to dispute Wolf's claim of self-defense, so the murder case got thrown out. They let him keep his job if he agreed not to sue the department. This guy is literally a wolf in sheep's clothing. It would be great press for us if we got the inside scoop on him."

"I'll think about it," Kahllah said flatly.

"That means you're gonna push it to the bottom of the pile and forget about it," Audrey said with an attitude. "So, you wanna do lunch later or what?"

"I wish I could, but I'm probably going to be tied up in meetings until God knows when. Maybe we can grab a late dinner tonight?" Kahllah suggested.

"Sounds good, but you're treating since I've been carrying your load and mine since you've been MIA." Audrey slid off the desk. "And Kahllah, at least give this Wolf situation some thought before you sweep it into the trash."

"I will, Audrey." Kahllah moved back over to her laptop to check her e-mail.

When Audrey took the hint and left the office, Kahllah picked up the newspaper and studied Detective Wolf's photo. He was a nice-looking man; in the photo he appeared a bit thuggish, but hardly the type for all those things Audrey was saying about him—though she knew it was always the ones you least expected. She rolled the newspaper up and tossed it in the trash before turning her attention back to the classified ad she had circled.

CHAPTER 4

DETECTIVE WOLF, THIS IS AN UNEXPECTED SURPRISE."
She was a bit older than he remembered. Her black hair had begun to thin and gray at the temples; crow's feet lined the corners of her eyes. If he recalled correctly, she ought to be somewhere in her mid-to-late thirties, but looked like she was north of forty. Stress and heartache could sap your youth faster than anything else, and Wolf knew that Edna Gooden had been through more of both than anyone should be made to endure.

"How're you, Mrs. Gooden?" Wolf asked.

She shrugged her thin shoulders. "I've been better and I've been worse, but I'm here, so I guess there's no sense in complaining. What brings you here? Have there been any new developments?" Her eyes looked hopeful.

The question stung Wolf and he wished he could tell her something other than the truth. "No, ma'am. I'm afraid I'm here about something different. May I come in?"

"I'm sorry. Where are my manners? Yes, please come in." Mrs. Gooden opened the door wide for Wolf to enter.

For the most part, the apartment was the same as he had remembered it: television mounted in an old-model entertainment system, green couches sitting on a brown rug. The only difference was that the apartment was far less tidy than it had been. Clothes were piled in corners between the couches, which he could tell needed to be washed from the slight moldy smell they produced. Empty beer bottles littered the table and an ashtray overflowed with cigarette butts.

"Excuse the mess, I've been busy working double shifts this week and haven't had a chance to straighten up," Mrs. Gooden told him, noticing how Wolf was looking around at the apartment. "Can I offer you something to drink?"

"No, I'm fine, thanks. I don't want to take up too much of your time. I just need to ask a few questions and I'll be on my way."

"Sure, detective. Please, have a seat." Mrs. Gooden moved some old newspapers off the couch. She took the spot on the sofa directly across from him. "How can I help you?"

"It's about the priest who was murdered last night, Father Fleming. I understand that you knew him?"

"Oh yes, John and I were members of his congregation. I was devastated when I heard the news. Have you come any closer to finding out who did it?" she asked.

"I'm working on it. Do you know anyone who could've possibly wanted to hurt Father Fleming?"

"I haven't a clue. All the members of the church loved him, he was a blessing. Lord knows, I have no idea what I'd have done without him to help us get through what happened to John Jr." Her eyes seemed to well with tears when she spoke his name. "That was a rough time for us . . . real rough. Sometimes when I hear kids running in the hallway I think John Jr. is going to come busting through the door and tell us this whole ordeal has been one big joke."

"I'm sorry if I opened up an old wound, Mrs. Gooden."

"It's okay, detective. It's been years and you would think I'd be able to talk about it without turning into a water bucket, but I still haven't been able to totally come to grips with what happened to my son. The worst part is not knowing. I'd give anything in the world to be able to look the killer in the eyes and ask him why. Why would someone do that to my baby?"

Before joining the narcotics task force, Wolf had cut his teeth as a detective working in the missing persons division. It wasn't exactly a dream assignment for the young detective, but what it lacked in excitement it made up for in reward. It did his heart good to be able to reunite families with missing loved ones, or at the very least

be able to give them closure—but with the good came
the bad. Wolf had been assigned to the case of a missing
boy named Johnny Gooden who had disappeared one
afternoon on his way home from a Little League game.
It would be months before Wolf was able to bring the
Goodens word of their son. He had been found in the
woods just north of the city, buried under snow and hidden until the spring thaw, still wearing his Little League
uniform. The cold had preserved whatever was left of
Johnny that animals hadn't picked over, which allowed
an autopsy to be done. Johnny had been beaten, sod-
omized, and eventually strangled to death before he was
dumped in the woods like trash. The horrible murder
was too much for Wolf, and after the case was officially
closed, he transferred from missing persons to narcotics.
The killing of adults he could deal with, but his heart
couldn't take the sight of another dead child. To that
day, Wolf could still hear Mrs. Gooden's screams in his
ears when he brought her the news of her son and pre-
sented her with the red baseball cap they'd found with
Johnny's body.

Holy shit, Wolf almost said out loud when the missing
pieces of the puzzle came together in his head. He now
remembered why the bloody baseball cap at the church
had caught his eye. "Mrs. Gooden, if I'm not overstep-
ping my bounds, could you tell me what became Johnny's

baseball cap? The one I brought to you and your husband the day we found him."

"It's hanging in his room, where it's been since you gave it to us. What does Johnny's cap have to do with the murder of Father Fleming?" Mrs. Gooden asked.

"Maybe nothing . . . maybe something. I just have a hunch that I want to follow up on. Could I see the cap, please?"

Mrs. Gooden was hesitant, but then she got up and went to the bedroom to retrieve the hat. While she looked, Wolf stood and moved to the mantle where pictures of the family were lined up. His eyes lingered on the one of Johnny Gooden and his father on the first day of Little League batting practice. Wolf examined the red cap in the picture and was almost certain that it was the same one he'd seen at the crime scene, but it didn't make sense. How could Johnny's death be related to the murder of the priest?

The front door opened and in came John Gooden Sr. He was a burly man with thinning hair, wearing work boots and a dirty shirt. In his arm he held a brown paper bag that clanked with the familiar sound of glass bottles, likely from the liquor store. On his heels was a skinny young man wearing oversized jeans, a teenager who could've been a mirror twin for John Jr. His name was Scott, if Wolf remembered correctly—he was Johnny's older brother. When Scott spotted Wolf he looked surprised, but John Gooden Sr. looked enraged.

"What the hell are you doing in my house?" John Sr. demanded.

Wolf extended his hand. "How are you, Mr. Gooden?"

John Sr. did not shake it. "I didn't ask for your useless-ass hand, I asked what you're doing in my house."

"Dad, just relax—" Scott began.

"You shut your damn hole," John Sr. barked at his son, before turning his attention back to Detective Wolf. "I thought I made it clear the last time you darkened my doorstep that I didn't ever want to see your face again unless it was to tell me that you've caught the piece of shit that killed my baby boy!"

Wolf could smell the alcohol coming out of John's pores and knew there was no rationalizing with a drunk, but he tried anyway. "Mr. Gooden, I know there's nothing I can say to ease your pain, but please believe me when I say I tried everything in my power to bring your son's killer to justice. Not one person in the department worked harder on that case than me and not a day goes by that I don't ask myself if I could've done more to save Johnny from what happened to him."

"You should've done more!" John Sr. snapped. "The pain of a parent having to bury their child is something I wouldn't wish on my worst enemy."

"I'm sorry," was all Wolf could say.

"Damn right you're sorry, you and the whole NYPD!"

"What's all the noise out here?" Mrs. Gooden returned from the bedroom. "John, why would you speak to a guest in our house like that? Apologize!"

"It's fine, Mrs. Gooden," Wolf told her. In all actuality, he wanted to put John Gooden on his ass for speaking to him in such a way, but out of respect for what he'd been through he held it together. "If I could just take a quick look at the baseball cap, I'll be on my way and out of your hair."

"Well, that's what I was coming to tell you. I can't seem to find the cap. I saw it on the wall in its usual place a few days ago, but when I went to look just now it was gone."

"You mean Johnny's Little League cap? Why are you snooping through my son's things?" John Sr. asked.

"Detective Wolf thinks he may have a lead," Mrs. Gooden answered for him.

"More like a hunch I'd like to follow up on," Wolf corrected her.

"Well, then you're too late. The cap isn't here anymore," John Sr. said, to the surprise of everyone in the room, especially Mrs. Gooden.

"What do you mean? What did you do with Johnny's things?" she asked frantically.

"A few days ago someone came around collecting clothes for homeless kids, so I donated a bunch of things the kids have outgrown and Johnny's cap," John Sr. confessed to his wife.

"How could you?" Mrs. Gooden was mortified. "The cap was one of the few things I had left to hold onto that reminded me of Johnny. You know how I felt about it!"

"I couldn't take it anymore," John Sr. began. "I listened to you go on and on about Johnny, and saw the pain in your eyes when you were trying to bring yourself to clean out his room, and it got to me. Every time I went into that room and saw Johnny's cap hanging on the wall, it reminded me of what happened. It reminded me that I failed to protect my son." He almost looked ashamed.

"I can't believe you would give Johnny's things away!" Mrs. Gooden shouted. She was starting to come unglued. She opened her mouth to say something to Detective Wolf, but the words caught in her throat. With tears streaming down her cheeks, she ran into the bedroom and slammed the door.

"Do you see what you've done? It's bad enough that you let our son die, but just when we're finally coming to grips with it you come back reopening old wounds!" John Sr. yelled at Wolf.

"Mr. Gooden, I didn't mean to make trouble. I'm only trying to help."

"You can help by getting out of my house and my life!" John Sr. raged.

"You got it," Wolf said, trying to hold his composure. John Sr. was hostile, and he wanted to match his hostility, but it wouldn't help his case. "Before I go, would it be too much trouble to ask if you remember the name of the organization you donated the clothes to?"

John Sr. gave him a look of disbelief, before taking two angry steps forward. Thankfully, Scotty stepped between them.

"Maybe you should go, detective," the young man suggested. He was a wise kid.

"Maybe I should," Wolf agreed. It was obvious that the Gooden home was a cold lead. Wolf gave John Sr. a last look, to let him know it was respect for his grief and not fear that was stopping him.

CHAPTER 5

WHEN DETECTIVE WOLF GOT OUTSIDE THE GOODENS' apartment building he felt more confused than when he'd gone in. It was obvious that the murder of the priest and the Gooden boy were connected, but without seeing how the baseball cap fit in he couldn't be 100 percent sure . . . and he needed to be certain before he could take any of his findings to the captain. And when that happened, what would the captain do with the information? Wolf had known Captain Marx for many years and he wasn't naïve enough to think that there wasn't more to the case than he was being told. Captain Marx was taking too personal an interest for it to just be about wanting to stop a rash of killings in his city. There was an endgame for him, and before it was all said and done Wolf would find out what that was.

"Detective Wolf," someone called from behind him. Wolf turned to see Scott Gooden coming out of the building. He had shed the doe-eyed look he'd had on his face in front of his parents and now wore a hard scowl. Even his oversized jeans sagged a little lower. He was the classic case of a kid living a double life: the good son in front of his parents, the cool cat in front of his homeys from the neighborhood. Wolf had played the same charade when he was a teenager toeing the line between good and evil.

"What up?" Wolf asked in a stern tone, not quite sure if the boy came in peace or wanted to pick up where his father left off.

"Yo, I wanna apologize for how my dad acted back there. He hasn't been the same since Johnny died. He can be kind of a dick sometimes," Scott said.

"So I've noticed."

"Well, the whole neighborhood has been talking about the priest. Once I heard, I knew the police would be coming by here to ask questions. Or at least I hoped."

"Scott, do you or your parents know anything about the priest's murder?"

"Nah, I don't know nothing about it, but I'm glad he's gone. I hated that muthafucka and he got what he deserved," Scott spat.

This surprised Wolf. "Those are some strong words about someone who you're mother seems to think was a good man."

"My mom's head is in the clouds. Father Fleming was a piece of shit and if you find the person who killed him, I'd like to shake their hand and tell them thank you."

"What's your gripe with the priest?"

Scott started to speak, but stopped abruptly when he saw the other teenagers who had been standing in front of the building watching him talking to the detective. Wolf noticed them too.

"I ain't no rat," Scott said. The tough-guy scowl was back.

"Scott, I know you ain't a rat. Anything you say will stay between us. You have my word on it. Now, it's obvious that you know something, so why not just tell me what it is. Help me connect the dots between this killing and your brother's murder," Wolf urged him.

"I never liked that dude," Scott began. "My mom and everybody else swore that he walked on water, but that's only because they didn't know him like we did. All of us kids hated him, except my dumb little brother. He was as blind to that snake as my mother and father."

"Did Father Fleming ever do anything to you? Did he touch you?"

"I ain't no fucking faggot," Scott snapped.

"I know you ain't no faggot, Scott. It's just a routine question," Wolf said. "Did you ever see him try and touch any of the other kids? Maybe your brother?"

"I would've killed him if I ever saw him messing with Johnny, but the way he used to look at him gave me the creeps," Scott answered.

"What kind of look? How did he look at Johnny?"

"Like he was a meal." Scott's voice was heavy with emotion. "He was always sniffing around Johnny, but he would lay off when me and the older kids were around. He knew we'd kick his old ass if he tried something. My mom would always make me take Johnny to his Little League games when my dad couldn't. The baseball field was only two blocks from the house and I didn't see why Johnny couldn't walk by himself, but my mother insisted that I take him. It pissed me off because when I had to watch Johnny, I couldn't run with my friends. So one day I told him to walk by himself, because I was trying to get busy with the girl form the third floor in the staircase. That was the day Johnny got snatched. It was all my fault!"

"Scott, you can't blame yourself for what happened to Johnny. You had no way of knowing that someone was going to kidnap him."

"But if I'd listened to my mom, it wouldn't have happened! She always warned me about looking out for my little brother and I fucked up. Now he's gone." Tears flowed down Scott's cheeks.

"And how does the priest play into all of this? What makes you think he was responsible for what happened to Johnny?" Wolf asked.

"I don't know for sure, but I felt it in my gut the moment he showed up at our house to lead the prayer circle for Johnny's safe return. There was something about him that didn't sit right with me. Everybody was all broken up about Johnny disappearing, and they were still hopeful that we'd find him alive—but not Father Fleming. He was talking about Johnny in the past tense as if he was already dead, before the body had even been found."

"How come you didn't tell me any of this when I was investigating the case?"

"I wanted to, but when I mentioned it in front of my mother, she slapped me in the face and told me it was bad to lie on good men. I should've said something anyway, but now it's too late. My brother's gone and there's nothing anyone can do about it."

"That's where you're wrong," Wolf told him. "If the two murders are connected, I'm going to find out. I told your parents years ago that I wouldn't rest until Johnny's murder was solved and I meant it."

Wolf's promise clearly made Scott a little hopeful. "Oh, and before I forget, there's one more thing." He pulled a folded slip of paper from his pocket and handed it to Wolf.

"What's this?"

"It's the receipt the guy who came to collect Johnny's clothes gave my father. He said something about it being a tax write-off."

Wolf examined the paper. It was from a standard receipt book that could be purchased at any stationery store. He was about to shove it in his pocket when his finger ran over the sheet and he felt grooves. "You got a pencil?"

Scott handed Wolf the pencil he had in his pocket and watched as the detective rubbed the pencil faintly over it. Just as he'd thought, there was something there. Someone had written something on the slip that came before it and left the impression. It was an address.

"Damn, where'd you learn that trick, at the police academy?" Scott asked, staring at the outlines of the numbers and letters that had appeared almost magically in the shadows of the pencil strokes on the receipt.

"No, reruns of the *Bloodhound Gang* on PBS." Wolf tucked the receipt in his pocket.

"The *what?*"

"Never mind. Thanks, kid. Is there anything you can tell me about the person who collected the clothes? Do you remember what they looked like?"

Scott searched his memory. "Yeah, he was wearing an army jacket. I remember because I thought the patch over the pocket was dope."

"What kind of patch?"

"It was a stork holding a rifle with some letters under it. I can't remember which letters, though."

"Thanks, Scott. You've helped more than you know." Wolf turned to leave.

"Detective Wolf," Scott called after him, "now that you've heard my story, do you believe me about the priest being involved or do you think I'm just imagining things like my parents have been saying?"

Wolf thought long and hard before responding. "I can't tell you what I think, but I can tell you what I *know*. And what I know is, if the two murders are connected, I'm going to find the thread that binds them."

CHAPTER 6

PONCHO PERUSED THE AISLES OF THE MINIMART inside the rest stop, thumbing through magazines and testing the air pressure on bags of potato chips. He'd spent the past twelve hours making deliveries and pickups between New York, New Jersey, and Pennsylvania, and was sick of driving. He couldn't wait to make his last drop so he could log out for the day and smoke a blunt and get some pussy that he didn't have to drive for.

Poncho felt like his most recent career path was well beneath his caliber and expectations. He'd had a good job working for the city morgue, where he made a nice piece of change and didn't have to do much work. Some people were squeamish about being around dead bodies all the time, but it didn't bother Poncho. He welcomed their silence, coming from a house with a nagging wife and four kids who he couldn't stand. It had been his perfect getaway, and the fact that he could come and go as he pleased without suspicion suited some of his extracurricular activities. He'd been able to feed the urges his wife couldn't satisfy. It had been the perfect job, but

Poncho had blown it all by doing a favor for a *friend*.

The sound of the door to the minimart opening drew Poncho from his moment of self-hate. A Latino family walked in, consisting of a squat father, a mother with eye-catching hips, and their two children. The oldest of the kids was a girl who looked to be about fifteen or sixteen with hips she had definitely inherited from her mother. From their tan lines and the way they dressed, Poncho knew they weren't local. They were likely passing through from somewhere warmer. The girl must've felt Poncho's gaze on her because she looked up and made eye contact with him. Poncho gave her a playful wink that made her giggle.

The father gave him a dirty look before barking something at his daughter and waving his hands in Poncho's direction. She said something back, then stormed off to busy herself at the soda cooler. The father looked like he wanted to continue the argument, but decided against it. He led his family to the other side of the rest stop where the food court and bathrooms were located.

Poncho watched the girl watching him through the cooler glass. He openly flirted and she was receptive to his advances. The tender young girl would be the perfect snack for his urge. After a brief look around to make sure the parents were nowhere in sight, Poncho made his move.

"*Como esta*, baby?" Poncho said, making it a point to sound extra-Latin. His Spanish was horrible, but he knew enough to make himself sound exotic when trying to run game on a girl.

This one just giggled.

"Such a pretty laugh to go with a pretty young thing. I'll bet when you take a shit, even your turds are pretty," Poncho said. It was a crass line, and a grown woman would've probably blown him off, but she was young and impressionable.

He stood there making small talk and laying compliments on the young girl, and she soaked it all up. She'd had boys come on to her but never a grown man, especially one as handsome as Poncho. She was putty in his hands. It took less than five minutes for the predator to talk the girl out of the minimart and into his van, which was parked around back.

The sun was already down, so it was dark out and nobody could get a clear peek inside the delivery van as long as he didn't turn on the dome light. The girl didn't speak much English and Poncho didn't speak much Spanish, but they both understood the universal language of marijuana. It was the promise of some primo choke that had been what sealed the deal. Poncho had gassed her up to smoke a joint with him in the van while her parents were still inside. What he didn't tell her was that he had laced the weed. Poncho slipped his hand in his pants and fondled himself, while the girl took deep tokes of the joint. She tried to offer it to Poncho, but he declined. He got so turned on watching her pink lips wrap around the joint that he couldn't help but to wonder how they would look wrapped around his dick. The visual became so intense that he almost blew his load in his pants. He and his urge would have to be patient. It only took a few minutes for the joint to start to take effect, disorienting the girl. She was finally primed and ready to feed Poncho's urge.

"Enough of sucking on that bud, chica, it's time for you to suck on some meat," Poncho said, pulling the girl toward him.

She tried to pull away, but the laced weed had her feeling like she had no control over her arms and legs. Still, she kept trying. When Poncho's palm landed heavily against her face she ceased her struggling. She was dazed, but she recognized the cold press of the knife Poncho had just laid against her throat.

"Listen here, you little bitch," he rained spittle in her face. "I planned to give it to you nice, but I'm fine with giving it to you rough if that's how you like it. Now, if you keep trying to fight me, instead of walking back in there to your parents, they're going to find you behind this minimart with your throat slit, *comprende?*"

The girl nodded.

"Glad we understand each other." Poncho set the knife on the dashboard and wiggled his pants down around his thighs so his dick could breathe. "Now, you get to sucking and you better not stop until my little man fills that pretty mouth of yours with joy juice." Poncho sat back and left the girl to her work.

Her tender hands felt like clouds caressing his balls and the shaft of his dick. He planned to make love to her mouth like it was his high school sweetheart. He could feel the heat from her mouth hovering above the head of his dick and his leg shook nervously in anticipation. But instead of feeling the soft lips of a young girl on his penis, Poncho felt a pinch.

He grabbed the young girl by her hair and pulled her head up. "Bitch, did you just nip my dick?"

The girl shook her head frantically, hoping he wouldn't hit her again.

Poncho was about to say something, when the pinch he felt on his dick turned into a throbbing, then graduated to a burning sensation. "What the fuck?" He hit the houselight so he could get a better look. Just over the vein of his dick there was a small bleeding pinprick. The flesh around the wound looked bruised and blackened. Poncho wasn't sure if he'd gotten a contact or not from being in the van with the laced smoke, but he could've sworn the bruise was spreading and turning his whole dick black. He grabbed the young girl by the neck and began shaking her. "You dirty bitch, what did you give me?"

"A little necrotizing fasciitis, spiked with the sap of a plant I crossbred with the hopes that it would accelerate the flesh-eating disease's process. From the pained expression on your face, I'd say it worked," a voice whispered in Poncho's ear.

Poncho looked up in the rearview mirror and saw someone sitting directly behind him, tucked in the shadowed recesses of the last few boxes he was supposed to deliver. He couldn't see the person's face because they were wearing a black mask, but in the center of the forehead of the mask was flower carved out of steel and onyx . . . a black lotus.

Ignoring the pain in his penis, Poncho shoved the teenager aside and lunged for the knife on the dashboard. His fingertips had barely grazed the hilt of the blade before pain exploded in the back of his hand. Embedded in the soft flesh was a hook, attached to a thin chain. He tried to reach with the other hand, but it too was snared. With a tug, Poncho was dragged onto the backseat. He tried to get up, but the chains pulled harder against him. Poncho lay on the floor of the van, arms spread like he was on a crucifix, at the mercy of the Black Lotus.

"Dear God," Poncho cried.

"God does not hear the whimpers of men like you, pedophile," the Black Lotus told him. "While busy adults turn deaf ears to the cries of wronged children, the Black Lotus hears them all." The killer straddled Poncho's chest. From a hip scabbard, the Black Lotus produced a flat blade that was nearly two feet in length. "Your kind are what's poisoning society, but I am the antidote."

"I'm connected," Poncho said nervously. "I've got some important friends who ain't gonna sit by and do nothing if you make me disappear."

The Black Lotus's head cocked to one side. "Isn't that what you've been doing, making people disappear? Yesterday it was evidence and today it's young girls. Does your evil know no bounds?"

Poncho's skin paled. "I don't know what you're talking about. I'm just a delivery guy."

The Black Lotus dragged the blade across Poncho's chest, tearing open his work shirt and a nasty gash just above his rib cage. "Your lies have no power over someone who has been shown the truth. My eyes have seen the glory and my ears have heard the voice of God. It was my Lord and Savior who sent me forth to slay the wolves and gather all His sheep so that they might hear His divine word too. Tell me, sinner, are you ready to hear the word?"

"Fuck you, you sick bastard. You're going to burn when word gets out about what happened to me. The people I'm connected to are gonna come around asking questions!" Poncho struggled against the hooks, only making his wounds bleed more.

"I fully expect them to ask questions, and when they do, my blade and His word shall be there waiting to answer them." The Black Lotus hoisted the knife above Poncho's thrashing body. "For the Lord Himself shall descend from heaven with a shout, with the voice of the archangel, and with the trump of God: and the dead in Christ shall rise first." The blade slammed into Poncho's gut. "Then we which are alive and remain shall be caught up together with them in the clouds, to meet the Lord in the air: and so shall we ever be with Him." The Black Lotus pulled the blade across Poncho's gut and stopped when it hit his breastplate. Then the killer angled the blade so that it was lined up with Poncho's heart. "Wherefore comfort one another with these words," the Black Lotus whispered before piercing Poncho's heart. "Thessalonians 4:16–4:18."

The teenage girl was curled in a ball on the floor under the dashboard, whimpering hysterically, trying not to look at the inky black form oozing toward her. Moving as subtly as a specter on a haunted breeze, the Black Lotus reached out and tilted the girl's chin up.

"Tsk, tsk . . . no need to fear the reaper, child," the Black Lotus said in an almost concerned tone. "Death comes for us all sooner or later, but I have no claim to your life . . . at least not tonight." The killer cupped the teenager's hands which, once released, were now holding a black lotus flower. "When you grow to be a woman and reflect on the blessings of your life, remember this night and who it was who gave you a second chance." Grazing the young girl's face with a gloved finger one last time, the Black Lotus turned back to Poncho, drew a short sword from a back scabbard, and began his work.

Only a few moments had passed, but it felt like an eternity before the teenager was able to finally find her voice and scream for help. Within minutes the local authorities had swooped in on the van. When they busted the window and pulled the doors open, none of them were prepared for what they found. The van was covered in so much blood that it looked like a butcher shop. On the floor of the front seat of the van, curled into the fetal position, they spotted the teenage girl, covered in blood and clutching a black flower.

CHAPTER 7

DETECTIVE WOLF HAD A BACKLOG OF CASES that needed tending to, but Father Fleming's murder nagged at him. He'd already had his suspicions about a few things, but the deeper he dug, the closer his suspicions danced to facts.

Scott throwing him the bone about the grabby priest could've just been the spite of a damaged kid, but Wolf didn't feel like it was. There was no mistaking Scott's disgust for Father Fleming, and it made too much sense for him to write it off as something fabricated by an angry teenager. Father Fleming was dead so there was nothing to gain from slandering him. Whether Scott's claims were fact or fiction, the teen believed every word he'd said.

Wolf decided to follow up on the address he'd found pressed into the receipt and it took him to Court Street in Downtown Brooklyn. He parked his truck in the taxi lane and hopped out, looking for the correct number, and found himself in front of a tall office building. In the lobby there was a newsstand and a bank of elevators that led to the offices on the upper floors. From the size of the building it would likely take him all night to find what he was looking for and he didn't have that kind of time. It was already after five o'clock and everything was shutting down.

Trying to figure out what to do next, Wolf stepped over to the newsstand to get a pack of cigarettes. He was all out and felt like he would be doing quite a bit of smoking while working this case. While he waited for the vendor to give him his change, a man came through the revolving doors. He was over six feet tall and powerfully built. In each hand he carried two large stacks of rope-bound magazines as easily as if they weighed little more than a carton of eggs. His strength was impressive, but Wolf was more interested in what he was wearing, a green army jacket with a patch over the breast: a stork holding a machine gun, with the letters *B. T.K.* beneath it . . . just like the patch Scott had described.

"Evening, Roger. Is that the new issue?" the vendor greeted the man.

"Yes sir, Mr. Suah. Fresh off the press." Roger smiled much like a child looking for his parent's approval. You could tell from the vacant expression in his eyes that he was missing a few cards from his deck. "I'm sorry I didn't get here earlier, but I had some other stops I had to make."

"No problem, Roger. I wasn't worried about it—you've never missed a weekly drop. Ms. El-Amin is lucky to have you."

"Nah, I'm the lucky one. She treats me real good," Roger said. He and Mr. Suah continued to make small talk, but Roger noticed that the man with the braids was watching him. "Something I can help you with?" he asked Wolf.

"I'm sorry, I didn't mean to stare. I was just admiring your jacket," Wolf said. "You a veteran?"

"Yes sir. Did a tour in Iraq."

Wolf stood straight up and saluted Roger. "Let me say that my family and I appreciate all that you troops do to keep our country safe."

"Thanks," Roger said, though clearly he was getting uncomfortable. "You want me to put these in the back for you, Mr. Suah? I gotta go."

"Sure thing, Roger. And thanks again," Mr. Suah replied.

"Hey, before you go, I'd like to ask you a question about your patch," Wolf interjected. "It means you served in some kind of special unit, doesn't it?"

"Something like that," Roger said in a dismissive tone.

"I figured as much. The only reason I asked is because I've been looking for a similar patch, in connection with a case I'm working on." He pulled out his badge. "Detective James Wolf—" he started, but never got to finish his sentence.

The man known as Roger swung one of the magazine stacks like a mighty hammer and caught Wolf square in the chin. Wolf felt the world spin, followed by his skull bouncing off the floor when he fell. Through dazed eyes, he saw the bottoms of Roger's sneakers as he made his escape. Then everything went black.

"Detective Wolf . . . Detective Wolf . . ."

When he opened his eyes, he found two uniformed officers and a paramedic standing over him. A small crowd had gathered around them, curious about what had happened.

"Are you okay, detective?" one of the uniformed officers asked.

"Yeah, I think so," Wolf said, rubbing his chin. From the way it throbbed he could tell without seeing it that it was swollen. He only hoped it didn't have too bad of a bruise.

"Do you think you need medical assistance, detective?" the paramedic asked.

"No, the only thing hurt right now is my pride." Wolf began climbing to his feet.

"You've taken a nasty blow to the head. Maybe you

should lie down for a minute." The paramedic tried to ease Wolf back down, but the detective pushed him away.

"If you don't quit trying to put me on the ground, *you're* gonna get a nasty blow to the head. I said I'm fine." At the newsstand, another uniformed officer was taking a statement from the vendor, Mr. Suah. "Who was that guy?" Wolf interrupted.

"It's like I was saying, his name is Roger. He delivers magazines for the company I order from. He's always very polite and I'm not sure what you said to him to set him off."

"What company does he work for? I need a name and address," Wolf demanded.

"I don't want any trouble. It's all right here." Mr. Suah handed him the invoice Roger had dropped off with the magazines.

"*Real Talk,*" Detective Wolf read the name out loud. He'd never heard of it, but from the mailing address listed he could see it was located in Harlem. He planned to pay them a visit and see about going another round with Roger, but his ringing cell phone said it would have to wait. "Detective Wolf," he answered.

"He's struck again," Captain Marx's nervous voice came over the phone.

"Damn, when?"

"About an hour ago, give or take. The ME says the body—well, what was left of it—was still warm when they arrived. This one is bad . . . real bad. How soon can you get to the crime scene?"

"Give me the address and I'll be there as soon as I can." Wolf listened as Captain Marx relayed the location. It was at a rest stop just across the George Washington Bridge. From the time of death Wolf was able to scratch Roger off the list of murder suspects. There was no way he could've killed someone then made it to Brooklyn to kick Wolf's ass in that amount of time. Still, he might not have been the killer but he was definitely connected in some way. When he found out how, he was going to nail Roger's ass, as well as everyone else connected with the murders, to the wall.

Wolf made hurried steps back to his SUV, which now had an orange parking ticket stuck to the window. It seemed like his day just kept getting worse. He tossed the ticket to the ground and jumped behind the wheel. As he was about pull out into traffic, he saw the familiar flash of a camera. He glanced around, expecting to see another nosy reporter trying to get pictures of him in a compromising position, but there was only a girl standing on the sidewalk, taking pictures of the park in front of the Supreme Court building. She was wearing a kebaya over dark jeans and her head was wrapped in a colorful scarf. Her big brown eyes stared at the building in amazement like she had just landed in Brooklyn from another planet.

"Fucking tourists," Wolf spat before merging with the traffic and heading to the crime scene.

By the time Detective Wolf arrived at the rest stop, it was already a media circus. Reporters hovered along the outskirts of the police barrier, buzzing and waiting for someone to let them in on what had happened. Between the media and the people who had been passing through the rest stop, it took the combined efforts of the state police and the local security to keep the crowd at bay.

He found Captain Marx standing just outside the police tape, talking to Detectives Brown and Alvarez. They were the last two people Wolf wanted to see. He was in no mood for their bullshit and had already decided that if Brown came at him sideways again, he was going to make him regret it.

"Captain," Detective Wolf greeted him with a nod. He didn't bother to acknowledge Brown or Alvarez, but he could feel their eyes on him.

"Thanks for getting here so quick, Wolf." Captain Marx shook his hand. He then turned to Brown and Alvarez. "You guys can go do what you gotta do. I need to talk to Wolf for a minute, but call me as soon as you turn something up."

"Whatever you say, *sir*," Detective Brown capped before leaving with Alvarez.

"I'd hate to be that sour muthafucka's partner," Wolf said once the detectives were out of earshot.

"I didn't call you here for your opinion of Detective Brown; I called you because there's another dead body lying at my feet."

"I'll be sure to shoot the killer a memo and ask if he wouldn't mind slowing down until I can catch up a bit," Wolf said.

Captain Marx's face turned beet red. "Let's see if you're still laughing when you see the size of the shit Black Lotus took in my lap." He ducked under the police tape, and motioned for Wolf to follow him.

Wolf had initially thought the minimart itself was the crime scene, but it was a van parked behind it. There were several medical examiners crawling in and out of the van wearing protective suits and carrying coolers. That was a bad sign. Captain Marx led Wolf around to the back of the vehicle where the doors were wide open. He smelled it before he even saw it. Not the smell of the decomposing corpse, but the blood.

Captain Marx had been spot-on when he said *butch-*

ered. Chains with hooked ends hung from the ceiling all through the van. On the ends of the hooks were body parts . . . an arm here . . . a foot there . . . The killer had hacked his victim to pieces and left him on display like a butcher's window.

"Who was this lucky bastard?" Detective Wolf asked.

Captain Marx gave him a look, but didn't feel like wasting his time reminding Wolf not to speak ill of the dead. "Delivery guy who worked for a private company in the Bronx. His name was Miguel Nunez, but they called him Poncho."

"Nunez? I know that name."

There was a visible twitch in Captain Marx's face. "You might. Before he drove a delivery truck he worked at the city morgue."

Wolf remembered now. Nunez was the creepy guy who handled the corpses before they made it up to the examiner's table. He had met the guy a time or two because he also handled the paperwork.

"So what makes you think it was our guy? I don't see any flowers," Wolf pointed out.

Captain Marx gave him another look.

"More misplaced evidence, huh?" Wolf shook his head. First a priest, and now a former morgue creep turned delivery boy, both dusted by a trained assassin. There was no way this was a coincidence. "Captain, was

Nunez working in the morgue when Johnny Gooden's body was brought in?"

"Detective, I need to keep your head in the present, not the past. This isn't about Johnny Gooden."

"Wrong. You made it about Johnny Gooden when you sent me to speak to his parents about Father Fleming. I think you knew that talking to them would reopen old wounds and light a fire under my ass to bust your little secret case wide open!" Detective Wolf said heatedly.

"If I were you, I'd watch your tone. I'm still your superior," Captain Marx shot back.

"Bullshit, this ain't about rank and respect, it's about *truths*, and I'm going to need some truth from you instead of the half lies you've been telling me since I signed up for this dummy mission," Detective Wolf barked.

Their raised voices were starting to draw attention.

"This was a bad idea," Captain Marx said, shaking his head. "That cold case was too personal to you and it's clouding your judgment about this live murder. I gotta pull you off this one."

"The hell you will!" Wolf shouted.

"Disobeying a direct order from a captain will be the nail in the coffin on your already shaky career, Wolf. Don't force my hand," Captain Marx threatened.

Wolf laughed. "You ain't gonna put me on the books for this one, Captain Marx, because if you do you'll have to explain to the brass why you've got a narcotics detective running a backdoor investigation on a homicide case. We both know you don't want that. You're not calling the shots on this one anymore, Marx."

"What are you saying to me, Wolf?"

"I'm saying that I'm going to solve these Black Lotus murders and finally give Johnny Gooden's parents some closure in the process." Wolf started for his truck. He stopped short with a few parting words for his old friend and mentor: "And captain, when I find out the truth I'm going to make sure all parties involved burn for it, regardless of which side of the badge they happen to fall on."

Captain Marx stood there, jaw clenched and fists balled angrily. When he had come to Wolf it had been out of desperation. He was the best tracker Marx knew, on or off the force, and would do the dirty deed with no questions asked. Or so Captain Marx had thought. He needed the Black Lotus stopped before he could finish his to-do list, and the Goodens were the only card he'd had to play without exposing his entire hand. But Wolf was a man who worked based on what he could gain, and there was nothing to be gained from reexamining the Gooden case. It was catching the Black Lotus that would make all his troubles go away, but obviously he had underestimated his former pupil's dedication to do-ing good police work.

Captain Marx went to his car and pulled a cell phone from the trunk. He punched in a number and waited for the person on the other end to pick up. "It's me," he said abruptly. "We might have a small problem."

Wolf was furious when he parted company with Cap-tain Marx. He stormed through the throng of report-ers, pushing, shoving, and in some cases snarling, as they tried to invade his personal space. The wise ones got out of his way and the foolish received elbows and trampled feet as he broke the media circle. He thought he had finally shaken all the vultures, until he got to his car and found one more waiting for him, leaning on the hood. This particular vulture he had seen before. She was still wearing the kebaya and jeans, but had shed the head scarf, letting her thick black hair hang free. When he'd first spotted her, he guessed her ethnicity as Middle East-ern, but now that he was getting an unobscured look at her face, he placed her as black or a dark Latina. It was the same girl Wolf had seen on Court Street in Brooklyn taking pictures.

"What are you, following me or something?" Detec-tive Wolf asked in a less-than-friendly tone.

"Actually, I'm following a story and you just happen

to be a part of it." She raised her camera and snapped a picture of him.

"Taking pictures of people uninvited can be bad for your health." Wolf gently pushed the camera away.

"And so can secrets," she countered.

"Who are you and what do you want?" Wolf asked, not liking what she was insinuating.

"My name is Kahllah. I'm a freelance journalist for *Essence* magazine," the lie rolled offer her tongue effortlessly. "What I want to know is, why is it that a narcotics detective is sniffing around a string of homicide cases?"

"I'm afraid you're mistaken. I'm not working the homicides. I'm just visiting a friend on the scene."

"A likely story, but at least you're not denying the homicides like everyone else." Kahllah smirked, tapping something on her iPad. "So, is it true that the recent string of murders are connected?"

"I don't know what you're fishing for, but you won't get it from me." Detective Wolf started walking around to the driver's side of his truck.

"Okay, if you can't tell me about these homicides, maybe you can help me fill in some of the blanks on another one. What happened the night Richie Dutton was killed?"

Detective Wolf's eyes darkened.

"I see that question got a reaction out of you," Kahl-lah said.

Wolf stalked back around the truck, nostrils flaring, and got in Kahllah's face. "Little girl, you don't know what the fuck you're talking about."

Kahllah was unmoved by his display of hostility. "You're right, I don't know what I'm talking about, but like any good journalist, I'm trying to educate myself. There are a few variations of the story, but in each of them you are fingered as the murderer of your partner. Care to comment?"

"Yeah, go fuck yourself." Wolf snatched her iPad and smashed it on the ground. As soon as he did so, he imme-diately regretted it. Some of the other reporters standing nearby quickly snapped pictures of the confrontation.

"Now that's going to make a nasty headline in some tabloid," Kahllah taunted him. "You can huff and puff like the big bad wolf all you want, but if there's a story here, I'm going to crack it. So you can talk to me will-ingly and put some truth on the table, or I can keep dig-ging and feed the public whatever I find."

"Little girl, you are skating on thin ice. If I were you, I'd be careful that it doesn't crack under your feet and land you in the deep end," Wolf threatened, before jumping into his truck. He peeled out of the parking lot, almost mowing down several reporters.

Kahllah stood there, smiling devilishly. Audrey had been right when she said an interesting story would come out of looking into Detective Wolf. He was volatile and rude, typical of a cop who was starting to crack under the stress of the job. With the right amount of pressure, he eventually *would* crack, and when he did, she'd be there to write about it—and whatever dirty little secrets he was trying to keep hidden.

The alarm on her cell phone went off, reminding her that she had an appointment to keep, so her investigation into Detective Wolf would have to wait.

CHAPTER 8

KAHLLAH FELT A CHILL RUN DOWN HER BACK when she crossed the threshold of the church. She had been raised in an Islamic home until she was captured by the slavers. Those men worshiped no God, and in those days the only thing Kahllah could find the strength to pray for was death. Her adopted father was a man of God . . . a Christian, and religion was a big deal in his house so Kahllah had embraced his faith. She'd been a member of this church's congregation since she was a teenager, and had spent many Sundays praying in their halls, though she still felt out of place. She navigated the carpeted aisle and stood before the stained glass mural of Jesus that dominated the wall behind the pew. She had loved it since the first time she saw it and could stare at it for hours. Something about it gave her peace.

Tearing her eyes away from the mural, she walked over to the confessional box. A man was coming out with an expression on his face that said he had just unloaded a heavy burden. She couldn't help but to wonder what sins he'd whispered. Was he a good man or an evil one? Would heaven be his last stop or hell? It was a game she and her friends at church would play when they were kids. They would watch the people coming out of the confessional and try to guess how deep their sins went.

Kahllah placed her green knapsack on the floor outside the confessional and stepped in. The booth smelled of musk and old wood. When she heard the screen to the adjoining window slide free, she crossed herself and laid down her burdens.

"Forgive me father for I have sinned," she began.

"How long has it been since your last confession?" the priest on the other side asked.

"One hundred and eighty-two days," Kahllah said shamefully.

"Why so long?"

Kahllah shrugged. "I guess I've just been busy with work."

"So, you're saying that there isn't enough room in your life for your career *and* your God?"

"No, I'm not saying that," Kahllah assured him. "In a sense, my work is for God. What I do helps a lot of people."

"A shepherd of lost souls," the priest said.

"I've never really looked at it like that, but it sounds about right. I encounter more than my share of lost souls . . . Sometimes it feels like too many."

"The Lord never heaps more on us than we can handle."

"I know, but sometimes it can be overwhelming. My best friend says I'm trying to save the world all by myself. I just wanna help those who can't help themselves," Kahllah told him.

"None but the Lord can save the world, but we can all do our parts to help the process along. Tell me, have you been doing your part?"

"Yes . . ."

"I detect some uncertainty within you."

"Father, I bust my ass from sunup to sunup for my cause. I'm not complaining, because I believe in what I'm fighting for, but to what end? It seems like for every wrong that I right, two more pop up in its place. The world is so full of wrong that I often find myself wondering when it gets easier."

"Never," the priest answered honestly. He was silent for a few moments before continuing: "The kingdom of heaven is like a man who sowed good seed in his field. But while everyone was sleeping, his enemy came and sowed weeds among the wheat, and went away. When the wheat sprouted and formed heads, weeds also appeared. The owner's servants came to him and said, *Sir, didn't you sow good seed in your field? Where then did the weeds come from?* He replied, *An enemy did this.* The servants asked him, *Do you want us to go and pull them up?* Then he answered, *No, because while you are pulling the weeds, you may uproot the wheat with them. Let both grow together until the harvest. At that time I will tell the harvesters: first collect the weeds and tie them in bundles to be burned; then gather the wheat and bring it into my barn.*"

"I'm afraid I don't understand," Kahllah said.

"In time you will. God will guide your steps through the weeds and lead you to the wheat. Say five Hail Marys and fast for a day. At the end of your fast your mind and your eyes will be refreshed."

"Thank you, father." When Kahllah stood up and left the booth, her knapsack felt a little heavier.

A few seconds after she had departed, the priest emerged from the confessional, smoothing his black robe. He was a hard-looking man, with a clean-shaven head and a salt-and-pepper goatee. Over his left eye he wore a black leather patch. "Too many lambs and not enough shepherds," he said aloud to himself before disappearing into the back of the church.

It was late when Kahllah pulled up in front of her Coney Island apartment building. She had a great view of the beach, though Audrey always asked her why she chose to live so far from where she worked; she didn't understand Kahllah's need for solitude. Much had changed with Kahllah since college and she valued her privacy.

She grabbed her purse and the green knapsack from the backseat and got out of the vehicle. A light wind tickled her face, whipping strands of hair across her forehead as she strolled from the curb to the brightly lit lobby of her building. The gray-haired doorman nodded to her, but didn't attempt to strike up a conversation. Everyone on staff knew that Kahllah wasn't big on conversation, though she rewarded them for respecting her privacy with envelopes stuffed with cash on the holidays. Kahllah smiled at the old man and continued on to the elevator.

On the twentieth floor she stepped out into the carpeted hallway. The walls were painted eggshell white with mahogany trim, to match the small coffee table in its center. The doors were all painted the same shade, with brass doorknobs. She proceeded down the hall and stopped in front of unit twenty-six. She unlocked her apartment door, but before opening it, she ran her hand along the edge of the frame. Neither of the pieces of clear tape she stuck in place every time she left had been disturbed. Some called Kahllah paranoid for the precautions she took, but she knew better than most the kind of evil that lurked in the world. Once she was sure it was safe, she stepped inside and engaged the multiple locks on the door behind her.

With the touch of a switch her living room was il-
luminated by track lights. It was tastefully decorated in
shades of cream and gold, giving it an old-world effect.
A leather sectional circled around the rear of the living
room, just in front of the balcony. On the left wall, there
was an entertainment system, housing a thirty-two-inch
television and a CD player. On the right was an oak
bookshelf that stretched from ceiling to floor.

Kahllah tossed her jacket over the arm of the wing-
back chair that sat against the wall by the door. She
would hang it up later. Kicking off her shoes, she made
her way to the sofa and placed her knapsack on her lap.
She rifled through the folders containing stories that she
was working on, and from the bag produced a thick ma-
nila envelope. She peeked inside and nodded in approval.
She removed a photo from the envelope and placed it
on the table. The envelope, and the cash inside, would
go into her wall safe later on, until she was able to get to
to her safe-deposit box at the bank. Kahllah never kept
large sums of cash in her apartment. The building staff
seemed honest enough, but she was a young woman, living alone, and there was no need to tempt fate.

She examined the photo, familiarizing herself with
the face. On the back of it were some notes written in
sloppy handwriting that Kahllah was familiar with, so it
wasn't hard to decipher the information. After commit-

ting everything to memory, she went into the kitchen and set the photo on fire. She dropped it into the sink, then leaned against the wall to watch it burn. When there was nothing left but ash, she rinsed it down the garbage disposal. Now she was ready for bed. She had a long day ahead of her and would need to be well rested.

Kahllah's sleep was anything but peaceful. She was plagued with nightmares as soon as she closed her eyes. The last one was the most intense. She dreamed that she was a young girl again, back at the hovel the slavers kept the girls in. She was curled up on a dirty cot, listening to the screams of a girl being raped in the next room. That night, just like every night she was there, she prayed for death, but it never came. A few minutes later, her door creaked open and several men walked in. It was her turn to be *conditioned*, as they called it. They wanted their girls to be tight for their clients, but not too tight, so they broke some of the fresher ones in.

She fought the men with everything she had but there were too many of them. Two of them bound her arms to the bed, while a third forced her legs open. Kahllah pleaded for mercy, but she knew that mercy was a foreign concept to these men. When one forced himself inside her, Kahllah felt like she had just been ripped in half. He did his business and freed his seed inside of her, before moving aside to let the next man have a go. Kahllah lay there, by now numb to the pain, and detached, while the men dripped sweat onto her frail body. She could still feel their rough mouths suckling her underdeveloped breasts. She wanted nothing more than to cry, but would not give the rapists the satisfaction.

There was a crash from somewhere behind them. Kahllah's vision was blocked by the man who was on top of her. There was shouting, followed by the sound of gunshots. Blood splattered everywhere, including in Kahllah's eyes. She tried to rub them clean, but it only made the blood seem to stick. She could feel herself be-ing snatched from the bed and the wind whipping past her face like she was falling from a rooftop. She closed her eyes, waiting for the impact of the ground below, but it never came. When she opened them, she was no longer at the hovel, but in a church.

She was older now, maybe about thirteen. She was wearing a pretty white dress and white Mary Jane shoes. She was on her knees before an altar, but she wasn't wor-shipping. Her arms were spread and tied to it. She struggled against the leather straps, but she was no match for them.

"The enemies of God are the enemies of His sword," she could hear someone behind her in the dream saying. *"Those who would stand against the one true God must be made to feel the sting of His blade."*

Fire shot through Kahllah's back as a whip was brought down across it. Blood now stained the arms of her pretty white dress and her back throbbed, but she knew this was only the beginning—it only hurt in the beginning.

"The will of God is the only law," the voice continued. *"Man has been corrupted and the wrong must be righted. Who has been chosen for this?"*

"The sword," Kahllah could hear herself saying in the dream. "The sword must cut the weeds so that the wheat may grow." Another blow fell across her back, but she refused to scream out.

"And it is the sword who has taken the sacred oath. It is the sword who has spoken the words before God and pledged to put the needs of man and the Lord in front of their own. Speak the words!"

Kahllah's lips moved but she could no longer speak. What were the words?

Another crack of the whip landed across her back. This one was so intense she felt like it had taken off her skin. She felt a strong hand grab a fistful of her hair and lift her head. Kahllah still couldn't see who it was speaking to her, but she could smell him. He wore the unmistakable smell of death like a designer fragrance. She could feel the cold touch of steel from the blade that was now pressed into her neck. *"Only the evil cannot speak the words. And as decreed by my Lord and Savior, the evil must be purified by blood and steel."*

This time Kahllah did scream. She screamed until her throat was raw and she was awake. Her eyes snapped open and she was on her feet and in a defensive stance before she could totally shake the sleep off. She looked around the room for the man who had been torturing her, but she was alone. There was no altar and no church; she was in her bedroom.

Her adoptive father once told her that the nightmares would fade, but she had yet to see evidence of that. The nightmares rode her like a dark horse and she doubted she would ever be free of them. Kahllah's body was still tired, but as hard as her adrenaline was pumping, she knew there was no way she would be able to make it back to sleep. She would likely be up for the rest of the night and through the day.

As long as she was up, she figured she would do something productive with her time. Slipping on a pair of sweats, a long-sleeved T-shirt, and running shoes, she headed out into the night.

CHAPTER 9

DETECTIVE WOLF TRIED TO GET SOME REST THAT NIGHT, but he couldn't. Ever since he'd left the Goodens' the case had been eating at him more than ever. There was something he was missing and he needed to find out what.

The way Captain Marx had reacted at the crime scene confirmed what Wolf had already suspected: the man had a personal stake in it. Wolf was sure that if he followed the threads of these crimes he would find the connections and see who all the players were, so he turned his living room into a staging ground for his investigation. There were pictures of different people, locations, and evidence from each crime. Files littered every flat surface in the house and his printer was working overtime. He imagined if he could figure out who the Black Lotus's next target was, he could beat him to it and lay this all to rest.

Wolf stood in the middle of his messy living room, examining the big board of information he had erected. In the center there were two pictures, one of Johnny

Gooden's dead body, and one of the priest's corpse. Each had lines drawn from them with marker that connected them to different photos. So far the players in the game who Wolf had identified were Mr. Gooden, Roger, Poncho, and of course Captain Marx.

Mr. Gooden was a mean son of a bitch when Wolf had first met him, and the murder of his son hadn't done much to improve his disposition. He had a violent temper and a drinking problem, so was it possible that he could've killed the priest? Maybe John Sr. had put more stock in his eldest son's story about the priest being a pedophile than Scott had known and paid Father Fleming a visit. He could see John Gooden Sr. after a long night of drinking confront the priest and things going south. Still, John Sr. was a brawler, not a butcher, and both victims had been butchered.

Then you had the late Father Fleming. Let the neighborhood tell it, he was a sweet old man who baptized babies and married young couples off, but Scott Gooden had a different impression of him. With all the stories Wolf had been seeing on the news about sexual abuse in the church, it didn't seem that far-fetched that Father Fleming could've been a predator. It was always the ones you least expected to have the ugliest secrets.

It took a simple phone call to confirm that Poncho had been working at the city morgue at the time Johnny's body was brought in and he was fired not long after. From what Wolf had heard about the man, the notion of him being fired for fucking corpses was plausible— and one thing working that case had taught Wolf was to take nothing at face value. It was his guess that the man's firing had nothing to do with necrophilia and everything to do with what happened to Johnny. He would've been the first one to come into contact with Johnny's body before it made it to the medical examiner's table and the last one to make contact with it before it was sent back down to the freezer. Was it possible that he had done something to make Johnny's death look like something other than what it was?

Roger was another story. From the way he'd taken off when Wolf asked about his patch, clearly he was hiding something. Wolf had reached out to a few people about the patch worn over Roger's jacket and found out that it was the insignia of an Army Ranger unit that called themselves Born to Kill, or B.T.K. for short. They were all whack jobs who did the dirty work behind enemy lines, no questions asked. Roger was without a doubt a killer, but not the Black Lotus killer. Even if it hadn't been for the conflicting times between the last murder and he and Roger's fight, he wouldn't have pegged the guy for the assassinations. He had the training, but not the mental capacity. The murders were skilled, and well thought out, and Roger was a half-witted brute. He had scratched the man from his list of killers, but he still wondered what his connection was. What or who was he hiding that would've made him risk assaulting a police officer, knowing he'd likely be caught?

Last but not least, there was the ringmaster of it all, Captain Marx. Wolf had known Marx almost all of his life. He knew Marx was a good cop, but he also knew that he was a man who didn't mind straying from protocol to manipulate the strings of justice. He had been like a surrogate father to Wolf growing up, but now he was a suspect. His reaction at the crime scene confirmed what Wolf had already suspected—that he was connected to all this somehow. The question was, how deep was he in it? Could it be possible that the man, who had taught him everything that he knew about the law, was pissing on it to save his own ass?

Wolf found a headache coming on from trying to answer all these questions, so he decided to take a break. He grabbed a beer from the fridge and flopped on his couch in front of his laptop to check his e-mails. In the spam folder he found a correspondence he'd been waiting for from the administrative department at One Police Plaza. He was banging one of the clerks, so he would call in favors from time to time. The e-mail had details about the Johnny Gooden case, such as chain of custody and the names of the officers working on it. Captain Marx had been a lieutenant back then and was spearheading the investigation. It was mostly information that Wolf already knew, so he was about to discard the e-mail when something caught his eye. One of the files included as an attachment had been submitted by a lawyer in the DA's office. It wouldn't have warranted a second look had Wolf not noticed her name, Margaret Stone.

Detective Wolf knew the name because every time he turned around she was in the newspaper. She'd had a promising career in law before abandoning it to run her husband Dirk Stone's mayoral campaign. Though her husband didn't win, Margaret's tireless efforts made her an overnight celebrity and a regular on the New York social scene. When she wasn't busy with her nonprofit organization, she was picketing abortion clinics and petitioning for better health care in inner cities. The woman was damn near a saint and it was surprising that her name would be attached to something so dirty.

Something about it nagged at Wolf, so he did a quick Google search of *Margaret Stone*. The usual stuff popped up about the mayoral campaign and her charity work around the city. One of the links led him to a website that had high school yearbook pictures of her. Back then she was a rather plain redhead with acne, and didn't look anything like the regal older woman she had become.

While scrolling through the pictures, one in particular made Wolf do a double take. It was a shot of Margaret dressed in a cheerleader's outfit. Her arms were draped around a beefy young man in a football jersey, kissing him on the cheek. He was more fit back then and had a head full of hair, but Wolf would know Captain Marx anywhere. It appeared that they had been high school sweethearts. That might explain his concern about the case: maybe he was covering for an old flame. The photograph gave him some new insight into the case, but it was the ID tag underneath that hit him like a slap. *Stone* was Margaret's married name. Before meeting her husband she had been Margaret *Fleming*.

CHAPTER 10

WHAT ARE YOU DOING OUT HERE, HONEY? Did the barking dogs wake you?" Dirk Stone asked, his voice thick with sleep. When he had awakened in the middle of the night to use the bathroom, he found her in the living room of their town house, staring out at the front yard.

"No, they didn't wake me, I just couldn't sleep," Margaret lied. She had received a very disturbing phone call earlier that day and had been rattled ever since, but she didn't want Dirk to worry. She kept her eyes fixed on the two male Dobermans that guarded their property. Something had them agitated. It was probably the neighbor's new poodle. Whenever the neighbor let the dog out and the Dobermans got a whiff, it seemed to make them crazy. They were typical males.

"If you want I could have Carl and Eddie put the dogs away for the night," Dirk offered. Carl and Eddie were the two bodyguards who lived on the property with them.

"The dogs are fine, honey. Leave them be. They're not what's on my mind," Margaret said.

Dirk walked up behind his wife, slipped his arms around her waist, and kissed her on the back of the neck. "Still thinking about what happened earlier? I keep telling you that when you're in the limelight you have to learn not to be bothered by the shenanigans of the media."

Earlier that evening Dirk had accompanied Margaret to a ribbon-cutting ceremony at a domestic violence shelter that her organization had helped to build. During the press conference there had been a journalist from some magazine who had been firing off some very uncomfortable questions. She seemed more interested in Margaret's time working in the DA's office than the ribbon-cutting ceremony. When she asked Margaret about accusations of evidence tampering and filing false reports, security had removed her, but the damage was already done. Soon the focus of the press conference shifted and they had to end it early. Margaret handled it with tact and grace, but her husband knew it had upset her.

Margaret placed her hands over his. "I know, but I can't help getting upset when people like that try and cast a negative shadow on the positive work I'm doing. I'm not perfect and I've made some mistakes in my life, but I'm trying to make a difference."

"You're doing more than trying, you *are* making a

difference. We're going to conquer the world, one opinion at a time. You wait and see," he promised, and sealed it with a kiss. "Now, come back to bed. I want to show you just how much I appreciate what you do." He tugged at the belt of her bathrobe.

Margaret allowed her husband to pull her closer, and they began kissing passionately. They were just about to go to the bedroom to finish what they'd started when she stopped suddenly.

"What's the matter?" Dirk asked.

"Do you hear that?"

"I don't hear anything."

"Exactly. The dogs have stopped barking."

"Maybe the poodle went back inside," Dirk suggested. As soon as the words left his mouth, they heard the gunshots.

"I hate those fucking dogs," Eddie said, taking deep drags off his cigarette.

"Me too. All they do is bark, but what are we gonna do? Bossman loves those mutts. He'd get rid of us before he got rid of them and I don't know about you, but I need my job," Carl said. He was leaning against the front of the house, watching the dogs and waiting for Eddie to finish his cigarette. The larger of the two Dobermans, Brutus, spotted something on the far side of the yard that sent him galloping away and barking his head off. Caesar, the smaller of the two, followed. "Where are those dumb-ass dogs going?"

"They probably spotted a raccoon or something. We'd better go get them before they get scratched. I don't want to be the one to have to take them to the vet for the rabies shots," Eddie said.

"Good point," Carl agreed. But before they could investigate where the dogs had disappeared to, the barking abruptly stopped. There was a low growling followed by two high-pitched yelps. Carl looked at Eddie and they were both wearing the same facial expression. Something was wrong.

"I'll take the point, you back me up," Eddie said, drawing his 9mm from its holster and venturing out into the darkened front yard. He and Carl crept across the lawn, weapons out and ready. Eddie turned to say something to Carl, momentarily not paying attention to where he was going. He tripped over something in the yard and fell face-first to the grass. When he looked to see what he had stumbled over, he found Caesar's lifeless eyes staring at him. Brutus was stretched out a few feet away. They had both been gutted and their intestines were spread over the grass around them.

The moment Carl's eyes landed on the murdered dogs, he began sweeping the yard with his gun. By now,

Eddie had made it back to his feet and was standing beside him. Something moved in the bushes and Carl opened fire without giving it a second thought. There was a shriek, letting him know his bullets had found their mark. With Eddie covering him, he jogged across the yard to see who or what he had hit. When he pushed the bushes aside, he discovered that he had killed the next door neighbor's poodle.

"Fuck," Carl said, peering down at the dead dog.

"Nice shot," Eddie said sarcastically. "Maybe next time you can—" His words were cut short and his eyes went wide. His mouth opened and closed like he was trying to speak, but instead of words, blood came out. There was a sickening sound of a blade being pulled from flesh, before Eddie's body fell to the ground. Standing behind him was a figure clad in all black, its face covered by a black mask. On the forehead of the mask was a black flower.

"The Black Lotus," Carl gasped. He had never met the killer, but he'd heard the horror stories about the assassin during his days of working Special Forces in the Marines.

"If you know my name, then you know the gift I bring," the Black Lotus spoke. The voice sounded mechanical and distorted as if coming from a navigation system.

"You take one more step and I'll blow that mask off your face," Carl warned. The Black Lotus stopped moving. "Now let me see those hands."

"Ask and you shall receive." The Black Lotus flung both hands forward like a magician casting a spell, and a chain appeared out of nowhere, streaking toward Carl. He managed to get off a wild shot, as one of the metal hooks bit into the back of the hand holding the gun. With a tug, the Black Lotus dragged the hook through the muscle and tendon of Carl's hand, rendering it useless and causing him to drop his gun.

Carl kneeled at the feet of the killer, clutching his ruined hand and staring up at him murderously. "If you want me to beg for my life, it ain't gonna happen. So do what you gotta do," he spat.

The Black Lotus pulled a black folding fan from a thigh scabbard and flicked it open so that Carl could see the razor-sharp metal where the paper folds should be. "Asking you to beg would be to give you a false sense that you might actually survive this encounter." In a swift motion the fan divorced Carl's head from his body. Kicking Carl's head along like a soccer ball, the Black Lotus started toward the house and his next target.

Detective Wolf's truck pulled to a screeching halt in front of the residence. Margaret Stone and Captain

Marx were the last two people on his list of players in the game, so he had given it a fifty-fifty chance that she would be the next target. From the bodies stretched out on her front lawn, he knew he had guessed correctly. One of the dead men there in front of the house was missing his head. It was definitely the work of the Black Lotus. He only hoped that he hadn't arrived too late to save Margaret Stone.

With his gun drawn, he made hurried, yet cautious steps toward the entrance. On the front steps he found the missing head, mounted on the banister with the skin of its mouth carved to make it look like he was smiling. The head looked like a jack-o'-lantern carved out of flesh. Wolf hoped that the carving had been done postmortem, because he hated to think of the pain the man would have felt if it were done when he was still alive.

The door was ajar and Wolf could see a smear of blood on the doorknob. Carefully, he pushed it open and crossed the threshold. Inside the foyer he found the body of Dirk Stone. His throat had been slit and a small .22 was clutched in his dead hand. From the look of things, he had tried to protect his wife when their bodyguards had failed and hadn't fared much better.

The sounds of struggling and breaking glass in the next room drew Detective Wolf's attention. As quietly as he could, he crept to the mouth of the living room and peered inside. Margaret Stone was on her knees, bloodied and beaten, but still alive. Hovering over her was the infamous Black Louts. The assassin held what looked like a short sword over the woman's head, prepared to deliver the killing blow.

"Don't move," Wolf demanded, aiming his gun.

The Black Lotus paused, and turned to the detective. "The infamous Lone Wolf James. I expected that our paths would eventually cross, but not before my work was done, detective."

"Well, I hate to piss on your parade, but this is a job that you won't get to finish. Put the blade down," Wolf said.

"I think we both know that's not possible. I have no claim on your life, but judgment has already been passed on this one. She must answer for the crimes she's committed."

"I can't let you do that." Wolf adjusted his grip on his gun.

"And I can't let you stop me," the Black Lotus shot back. "Put down the gun, detective, or she dies." The Black Lotus adjusted the blade at her throat.

"Okay, just don't do anything rash." Wolf slowly bent down and put his gun on the floor.

"Now kick it away," the Black Lotus ordered.

Detective Wolf reluctantly complied. "Why are you doing this?"

"The fact that you've come here means that you already know. She, like the rest, must atone for her wrongs. They are the unclean and I am the purifier."

"Please, I don't know what you think I've done, but I haven't. You're making a mistake," Margaret Stone spoke up.

"The hand of the Divine is without flaw when guiding the sword of justice," the Black Lotus snarled, applying enough pressure to the blade at her neck to draw blood. "For there is nothing hidden that will not be disclosed, and nothing concealed that will not be known or brought out into the open."

"Luke 8:17," Detective Wolf blurted out.

This gave the Black Lotus pause. "You're a believer?"

"At one time, I guess you could say that I was. I spent a lot of time in church as a kid. These days I'm not sure what I believe in outside of justice."

"If you believe in justice then you of all people should understand what I must do here. She's got to pay for what she's done."

"I keep trying to tell you that I don't know what you're talking about," Margaret pled.

"Liar!" the Black Lotus raged, and delivered a vicious slap across her face. "Is that what you tell yourself so you can sleep at night? Your lies will end today, and the sword of God shall prevail where the law has failed. Justice must be done."

"And what does a mercenary know about justice?" Wolf asked, gradually inching forward.

"Is that what you think I am, a common assassin for hire?"

"That's why you're doing this, isn't it? The Black Lotus sells death to anyone who can afford it."

"You're right, I am paid to take lives, but this killing has nothing to do with money. This contract was paid for in suffering, which I intend to inflict on Margaret for her role in what happened. You are blind to the truth, detective, but I see it clearly."

"You can't hold her accountable just because she's related to the priest who killed Johnny," Wolf said, to the surprise of Margaret. She'd thought her secret safe. "Yeah, I know that you're a relative of Father Fleming and that you signed off on the paperwork that tanked the case. You'll get what's coming to you, but not like this." He turned his attention back to the Black Lotus. "The priest and the others who were involved are dead. I'd say the scales are balanced. Why don't you let the lady go?"

The Black Lotus laughed. "It's obvious that you've only found some of the pieces and have not yet assembled the puzzle. If you had, you wouldn't be trying to stop me from killing her; you'd be fighting me for the honor of doing it yourself. Would you care to fill him in, Margaret?"

"I never touched that boy, I swear," Margaret sobbed.

The Black Lotus slapped her again. "No, but you ushered the lamb to the wolves. Tell him!"

"What's he talking about?" Wolf asked.

"I was only trying to protect him," Margaret finally broke down. "My father had always had a thing for young flesh. He never touched me or my brothers and sisters, but we heard stories about things he was accused of doing to other kids in the neighborhood—that's why we moved around so much. Every time we'd get settled someplace, his urges would come back and the rumors would start. When we were older, my brother and I found a way for my father to satisfy his needs without anyone getting hurt. You'd be surprised how many street kids willingly sell their bodies for a few dollars and a hot meal. For a while I thought we had it under control—until I heard Johnny Gooden disappeared. My father could be rough some-times, but never truly violent. I didn't want to believe he had done it, but the minute I asked him about it and saw the look on his face, I knew. I called in some favors and directed all the attention away from my father. I swear, on everything that is holy, not a day goes by when I don't think about Johnny Gooden, and it killed me knowing I played a part in burying the case. I knew my father was a sick man, but he was still my father and I loved him."

Wolf shook his head in disgust. Helping to sack a few cases, he could understand, because he had done it more than a few times. But her knowingly feeding her father children to hurt wasn't something he expected to hear. He had a good mind to let the Black Lotus finish her, but he was still a peacekeeper and had taken an oath to enforce the law. "And what about your old boyfriend, Captain Marx? What part did he play in all this?"

Margaret looked confused. "Tommy wasn't my boyfriend, he's my half brother. We didn't know about each other until sophomore year in high school when he moved to New York. He was the product of one of my father's first victims. It was him who came up with the idea of feeding Daddy the child prostitutes."

Just when Wolf thought the case couldn't get any stranger . . . He had known Captain Marx nearly all his life. Growing up he had come to love and respect the man like a surrogate father, yet it was clear now that he was nothing more than a monster like the rest of them. Suddenly he felt very, very ill.

"And there you have it, detective. So now you understand why she and the rest were marked for death," the Black Lotus told him.

"If they're guilty then let me bring them in. Let the law handle it."

"Sadly, I have lost faith in the law, detective. This

is God's will, and so it shall be done." The Black Lotus gripped Margaret's neck to prepare for the killing stroke, and it was then Margaret made a last desperate attempt to save herself by sinking her teeth into the killer's hand. The Black Lotus let out an oddly high-pitched scream. Margaret scrambled away, giving Wolf the opening he needed.

He launched himself across the room and tackled the Black Lotus, sending them both flying into the china cabinet and knocking away the blade. With both of them now unarmed, the fate of Margaret Fleming Stone would be decided by a good old-fashioned fistfight. The two combatants stalked each other, throwing jabs and feints, testing each other's defenses. It was Detective Wolf who grew impatient and struck first. He launched a combination of punches at the assassin's head. The Black Lotus moved faster than anything Wolf had ever seen, dodging the punches and countering with a straight jab to the detective's mouth. He stumbled backward, blood spilling onto the carpet.

"You're making a mistake trying to stop me, Detective Wolf." The Black Lotus danced like a boxer.

"No, I'm not. For once in my life I'm doing the right thing. You wanna get to her, you'll have to go through me." Detective Wolf placed himself between the Black Lotus and Margaret.

"So it shall be done." The Black Lotus launched at Wolf.

As they grappled, Wolf noticed that the Black Lotus was surprisingly lighter than he'd expected. The killer's arms were coiled wires of muscle, but he had a very slight build. Wolf was able to use his weight against the assassin and press his attack. He hurled nonstop punches and his adversary backed into a corner. The Black Lotus's defense was good, but Wolf was tireless in his attack. A powerful right hand broke through, knocking away the iron mask. The head and lower half of the killer's face were still protected by the black cowl beneath the mask, but Wolf glimpsed eyes that were soft, brown, and familiar.

For a split second Wolf hesitated, and that was all the time the Black Lotus needed to strike out with index and middle fingers, jabbing the detective in the center of his chest. Wolf gasped, as it felt like all the air was being pushed from his constricting lungs. He continued to try to fight, but his blows were slower and less coordinated. He threw an awkward overhand right, which the Black Lotus sidestepped, sending him crashing into an end table. The Black Lotus pulled Wolf to his feet, only to throw him face-first into the far wall of the living room, right next to the picture window.

Detective Wolf's legs felt like noodles, but he forced

K'WAN

INFAMOUS

himself to stand. His bloody lips drew back into a sneer. "Is that the best the Brotherhood of Blood has got? It's no wonder you sons of bitches are damn near extinct."

"Let's see where that wit of yours is when I make you bleed out on this carpet." The Black Lotus drew three stilettos from some hidden compartment in his clothes.

Wolf stared at the blades. "Weapons against an un-armed man? I thought your order had some code of honor," he said, moving out of arm's reach and closer to his gun, which was still lying on the floor.

"Honor went out the window when you threw in your lot with child murderers," the Black Lotus countered before advancing with the stilettos.

Just as the Black Lotus moved in to finish him, Wolf lunged for his gun. He slid across the floor on his back, arms outstretched and hope in his heart. His fingertips had just made contact with the grip of his weapon when one of the stilettos was plunged through the palm of his hand, pinning it to the floor. The Black Lotus straddled Wolf's chest, forced his other arm out so that his palm was exposed, and drove the second stiletto through it, stretching him out like Jesus on the cross.

"Stupid . . . just stupid." The Black Lotus kicked the gun across the floor and straddled Wolf's chest, holding the remaining stiletto over him. "You should've let me do my work. You came to be a martyr, so a martyr you

133

shall be." The killer plunged the last stiletto into the detective's stomach.

Wolf could neither move nor cry out. He simply lay there, feeling himself bleed out, just as the Black Lotus had promised. Wolf had often wondered what, if anything, people experienced when they died. Was there some great light at the end of the tunnel, or was it a quiet nothingness? From the numbness setting into his fingers and toes, he knew it wouldn't be long before his curiosity was satisfied.

Several small explosions erupted somewhere in the distance. Through his haze of pain Detective Wolf could see the Black Lotus staggering as another explosion sounded and the killer was knocked through the large picture window.

Lifting his head as best he could, Wolf saw Margaret standing in the middle of the room, frightened and disheveled. In her hands she held his smoking .45. The woman he had tried to save from vigilante justice had extracted a bit of justice of her own. One evil had trumped the other and the game had come to an end. Part of him wanted to kiss her on the lips for saving his life, and the other half wanted to handcuff her, but he was too weak to do either. A chill ran through his body, landing in the pit of his stomach and gradually spreading through his limbs and face. He was cold and just wanted to sleep, so he nodded off into sweet oblivion of the afterlife, knowing that in its own twisted way, karma had sorted everything out.

CHAPTER 11

WOLF WAS SITTING BEACHSIDE IN ST. THOMAS, sipping rum coladas with half a dozen local beauties. One of them was feeding him strawberries from between her breasts when his dream was interrupted by a flash of light. Wolf blinked, and the dream faded, with his beach chair and white sands being replaced by a hospital bed and white walls. There were multiple tubes snaking from beneath the flimsy blanket covering him, connecting to monitors which kept track of his vital signs. His hands were heavily wrapped in gauze, and though he could wiggle his fingers, he couldn't feel them. An oxygen mask covered his nose and mouth, helping him to breathe. When he tried to move, pain shot through his gut and he remembered that he had been stabbed, and everything else came back to him. He was in bad shape, but considering what could've been, he had come out on top.

As the fog rolled back from his mind and his vision cleared, he could see two people standing over him. One was Captain Marx; the other was holding a camera and kept snapping pictures of him. Every time the bulb flashed, his eyes stung a bit. Sensing his discomfort, Captain Marx dismissed the photographer and closed the door behind him.

Marx strode to Wolf's bedside and pulled one of the hospital chairs over. He sat down and for a few long moments, he and Wolf just stared at each other. When he felt like the pissing contest had gone on long enough, he spoke.

"How you doing, Jimmy?"

"How does it look like I'm doing?" Wolf's tone was labored and his voice muffled by the oxygen mask, but his irritation was apparent.

"Yeah, you were in pretty bad shape when they found you. The doctors say had it not been for Mrs. Stone's quick thinking and keeping your wound compressed, you'd have likely bled out."

"Remind me to thank her when I arrest her ass," Wolf said.

"Is that any way to talk about the woman who has made you a national celebrity?" Marx asked, holding up the newspaper that had been tucked under his arm so Wolf could read the headline. *Hero Cop Foils Assassination Attempt*. On the cover was a picture of him when they had first brought him into the hospital. Also in the picture was Margaret Stone. She was kneeling at his bedside surrounded by a dozen uniformed police officers, all with their heads bowed, while she led them in prayer for their injured comrade. The story detailed how one of the girls who Margaret's organization had been helping was an informant on a drug case Detective Wolf had been working. When he came to the Stone residence for a scheduled meeting with the young woman to take her statement, he had stumbled upon the crime scene. Dirk Stone had already died by the time he arrived, but he was able to stop the attempted assassination of Margaret Stone, almost at the cost of his own life. The story included a quote from Margaret Stone: *"This man is a hero and a saint. He should be given a medal for what he has done not only for me and my girls, but for the city of New York."*

Detective Wolf shook his head. "What a load of bullshit."

"You and I both know it, but the general public only knows what the media feeds them, which is best for all parties involved. On the upside, we managed to catch the priest's killer," Captain Marx explained. He flipped to the next page of the article which told the tale of a rash of murders that had been happening around the city over the past few days. They even had a picture of the culprit. Corporal R. Braddock was ex-military and connected to a black-ops unit that had done some nasty things while behind enemy lines, all in the name of serving their country. During his second tour of duty, Corporal Braddock had suffered a severe head injury and was honorably discharged. Yet when he came back from the war, he found himself, like many other veterans, displaced and left to fend for himself. Braddock looked different dressed in a military uniform, clean shaven and alert, but Wolf recognized the man he had come to know simply as Roger.

"Roger isn't the Black Lotus and you know it," Wolf groaned.

"Yeah, but the evidence says differently. We found Roger in a van a few blocks away from the crime scene. He put up one hell of a fight, taking out three of ours before blowing his own brains out. Poor bastard had no plans on going to trial with this. When we tossed the van, we found the murder weapon that had been used to kill both the priest and Poncho. The only prints on it were Roger's. The city is safe again, you get your promotion, and I take early retirement, going out as the man who stopped the biggest serial killer since the DC sniper. Everybody wins."

"Everybody except the family of the boy whose murder you helped cover up," Detective Wolf said, surprising the captain. "I know about you, Margaret, and the priest, Tommy. You taught me everything I know about being a cop. You're the one who showed me that putting my ass on the line night in and night out was worth it because of the good we do on the streets, but you're a fraud like the rest. I watched you piss all over the same badge you always told me to honor and respect."

"Don't you dare judge me for making the hard calls," Captain Marx snarled in Wolf's face. "For thirty years I risked my life for this city, even took several bullets, all in the line of duty. I never once complained about it, because it's what I signed on for when I took the oath to serve and protect. It's war on these streets and they're winning, so sometimes you've got to make your own rules to balance things out between us and the scum. You of all people should understand that. How many times have you bent the rules to get the job done?"

"Yeah, I've bent the rules more than a few times, but I've never broken them, and that's what you did when you thought it was a good idea to feed children to a pedophile," Detective Wolf shot back.

Marx shrugged. "We're all guilty of making poor decisions when it comes to family. My dad was a pervert and your dad was a junkie, but no matter how fucked up our parents were, there will always be parts of us that still seek the approval a son can only get from a father. Those kids were selling ass anyhow, so after a while I convinced myself that if it wasn't me paying them, it'd be somebody else. Johnny Gooden changed all that. After we helped to clean that mess up, we cut all ties with that sick old bastard. To be honest, I was relieved when he was killed. It meant I didn't have to worry about him hurting any more kids."

"Then why send me after the Black Lotus instead of tanking this case like you did Johnny Gooden's?"

"Once I realized that the Black Lotus was the one who had killed my father, I knew it could've only been because of what happened to Johnny. And if someone had set the Black Lotus to the task of making things right, I figured it would only be a matter of time before the rest of us were paid visits. I needed an insurance policy and you were it."

"How?"

Marx chuckled. "That should be obvious considering the outcome of your meeting. You and the Black Lotus have more in common than you think. You're both self-righteous and volatile, neither of you budge on your principles, and both of you will go the extra mile to get your point across. I never expected you to arrest the Black Lotus, I expected you to *kill* him."

"Your own personal attack dog," Detective Wolf said, with the pieces finally starting to fall into place.

"Send a killer to stop a killer."

"We both know that Roger isn't the Black Lotus, so the assassin is still out there. What's to stop him from finishing the job and taking you out?" Wolf asked.

"We have the late Mr. Dirk Stone to thank for that. He had a five-million-dollar life insurance policy with Margaret as the sole beneficiary. One million of that will be paid to the Brotherhood. That should be enough to buy out the Black Lotus's contract and compensate for any inconveniences."

"You've got it all mapped out, huh?"

"Advanced planning is why I was able to survive thirty years of policing New York streets."

"You know I'm going to come after you and your sister for the parts you played in covering up that boy's murder. This isn't over," Detective Wolf vowed.

"Oh, but I think it is," Captain Marx countered. "Everyone is satisfied with this outcome. Lots of innocent people got hurt from digging up old graves the first time around and we don't want a repeat of that. No telling how far the innocent bloodshed will spill this time and who it will affect, maybe even that pretty daughter of yours and her mother down in Florida."

Detective Wolf removed the oxygen mask from his face and stared Captain Marx in his eyes. "You threatening me?"

Marx patted Wolf's bandaged hand. "You're family, I'd never threaten you. I'm just telling you that you should pick your battles, Jimmy. Now, when you're feeling up to it, the chief is going to pay you a visit, bringing a bunch of reporters with him. You're going to give them some bullshit speech about how thrilled you are to be a public servant, accept your promotion and your commendation, and consider your sketchy-ass career started over with a clean slate. No more, no less. I'll be right here with you to make sure you stick to the script." He stood to leave. "It's already done, so fighting it is only going to hurt you." He tossed the newspaper onto Wolf's lap. "You can hold onto that in case you wanna brush up on the story you're going to feed the media. I'm getting out of here so you can spend some time with your girlfriend."

"My *who?*"

"Your girlfriend," Captain Marx repeated. "She's been here every day since they brought you in. With all due respect, that's one fine piece of ass. I'm proud of you, kid." He winked and left the room.

Detective Wolf had no idea who Captain Marx was talking about. A few seconds later, it became clear when the woman walked into the room. She had changed her appearance yet again, this time dressed in tight jeans, flat shoes, and a T-shirt that read, *Vote or Die*. Her dark hair hung loose around her face, though it appeared not to have been combed that day. She still had that bright inquisitive look in her eyes she'd had when they'd last confronted each other, only some of the luster was gone.

She seemed tired and was limping slightly. Hugged to her chest she held an iPad, almost identical to the one he had smashed in the parking lot.

"You got that replaced pretty quick." He nodded at the iPad.

Kahllah shrugged. "What can I say? Apple has a great protection plan. Do you mind if I sit?" She gestured at the chair Captain Marx had vacated.

"I have a feeling that even if I say no, you're gonna do what you want anyhow." Wolf watched as she pulled the chair close to the bed and eased down into it. Her movements seemed pained. "First you were a writer for *Essence* and now you're my girlfriend? Do your lies ever get you what you want?"

"There is a fine line between lies and truth and that all depends on who you ask." She leaned over and tapped the bottom corner of the newspaper article the *Daily News* had run about Wolf. The writer was listed as *K.E. Amin.*

"You wrote this article?"

"One of my many pen names," Kahllah replied. "I told you that if there was a story hiding beneath all this, I would find it and bring it to light."

"Then you should change the batteries in your flashlight," Detective Wolf laughed. When he did, his body was rocked with pain from his wounds. Once the pain had passed, he was able to speak again. "You need to recheck your facts."

"Oh, I'm well aware of the facts, detective. I know all about Johnny Gooden and the Black Lotus. I've done my due diligence, but I decided that in the end it was best for me to give the public what they want as opposed to what they need."

"So they've got *you* in their pocket too?"

Kahllah laughed. "I'm claustrophobic, so being in anyone's pocket would never work for me. I'm just a journalist who went in search of some truth."

"And did you find it?"

Kahllah paused before answering. "I'd say so."

"Would you care to share?"

"I could write a novel on everything I've learned, but I'll give you the meat and potatoes of it. Good people can sometimes be put in situations where they have to do bad things in order to really make a difference."

Wolf nodded, digesting what she had just said. "That makes sense."

"Well, I don't want to take up too much of your time because I know you need your rest. I just wanted to pop in on you and kind of apologize for the way I came at you the other day about the Richie Dutton thing."

"Wow, you don't strike me as the apologetic type," Wolf said.

"I'm not, but I'm not too stubborn to admit when I was wrong about something, and I was wrong about you."

"So you don't think I'm a killer anymore?"

"Oh, I know without question that you are a killer, Detective Wolf, just not a cop killer."

"And how do you know that?"

"Because you're one of the few who still believes in justice." Kahllah gave him a wink. "Take care of yourself, detective." She patted him on the leg and for the first time he noticed the bandage on her hand.

"What happened?" he asked, gesturing at the bandage.

Kahllah looked down at her wrapped hand. "My boyfriend likes to play a little rough sometimes. I've suffered worse, so I'll be okay." She turned to leave, but Wolf stopped her.

"Kahllah," he called after her, "one last question before you go."

"What's that?"

"Well, since you said you know about the Black Lotus, I'm sure in your quest for truths you were able to gain some insight on him."

"A bit . . ." Kahllah said hesitantly.

"When he and I spoke at Mrs. Stone's house, I got the impression that this little murder spree was about more than money. If not for money, what would make an assassin of the Black Lotus's caliber risk so much for those people to die?"

Kahllah gave him a half smile. "A mother's tears. Get well soon, detective," she said, and slipped from the room.

EPILOGUE

Two weeks later

FOR THE FIRST TIME IN WEEKS THE WEATHER HAD WARMED UP. It was a nice Saturday afternoon in the neighborhood. Kids were out playing, while adults came and went, handling this and that. Mrs. Gooden pushed her shopping cart of groceries, with her nose buried between the pages of a small Bible.

"Afternoon, Mrs. Gooden," a voice startled her from her reading.

She looked up and was surprised to see Detective Wolf standing there in front of her. He had traded in his sweat suit and gold chain for a blazer and tie. "Oh, I didn't see you."

"I've been learning to walk kind of light these days," he joked. For the most part he had recovered from his wounds, but his side still gave him some pain, causing him to limp a bit.

"I heard what happened to you and I'm sorry," Mrs. Gooden said.

"It's just a hazard of the job, I'll be fine."

"Where are you off to all decked out?" she asked.

"I have to go down to the office to fill out some paperwork. I'm supposed to start my new position next week. I'm now *Sergeant* James Wolf."

"Well, congratulations. So what brings you to this neck of the woods?"

"You, actually. I was wondering if I could ask you a couple of quick questions."

"Do we have to do it now? I've got ice cream in the cart for Scott and I don't want it to melt."

"No problem, I'll walk with you. This shouldn't take long." Detective Wolf fell in step with Mrs. Gooden. "You know, I felt horrible about coming to your house and stirring up those old memories. I didn't mean any disrespect."

"I understand that you were just doing your job, detective, but you'll have to excuse John for the way he reacted. He has just been so angry at the world since Johnny was killed."

"I can't say that I blame him. Losing a child is enough to turn even the most docile man into a powder keg. I know it had to be even harder on you."

Mrs. Gooden shook her head sadly. "You don't know the half of it, detective. There are days when I go sit in Johnny's room and just cry and cry."

"That bedroom is probably one of the few places you can go to still feel close to Johnny, huh?"

"John says I turned it into my own personal shrine. I think I spend more time in there than I do my own bedroom."

"I figured as much, which is also what got me to wondering about a few things."

"Such as?"

Detective Wolf stepped in front of the cart, causing her to stop. "Such as, if you spend so much time in Johnny's room, how come you didn't notice that the baseball cap had gone missing until I asked about it?"

She seemed dumbfounded by the question. "I . . . I don't know, I guess I just overlooked it."

"That's possible, but I doubt it. You said at the house that it was one of the few things you had to remember Johnny by, so I don't think you would've overlooked it disappearing. I think you orchestrated the cap's disappearance, among other things."

"Detective, I'm not sure I like the direction this conversation is going in. Now, if you'll excuse me." Mrs. Gooden tried to move around Wolf, but he blocked her path again.

"The first instinct of a guilty party is always to flee."

"Detective Wolf, are you insinuating that I had a hand in my son's death?"

"No, but I'm willing to bet this shiny new badge of mine that you hired the assassin who avenged it."

"That's impossible. Neither me nor my husband has any money, and whatever savings we had were used to pay for Johnny's funeral. What could I use to pay an assassin when I barely have a dime to my name?"

"A mother's tears," Detective Wolf replied. These had been Kahllah's parting words and they provided him with the final clue he needed to unravel the mystery. "The suffering of a woman grieving for her child is what set this all in motion, not money. I can speculate on what happened, but I'd rather you just tell me the truth."

Mrs. Gooden slumped over the handle of her cart, as if she were a balloon that had just been deflated. When she looked up at Wolf, her face was streaked with tears. "I just couldn't take it anymore," she began. "Scott told us about him suspecting Father Fleming being involved with what happened to Johnny, but of course neither me nor John wanted to believe him . . . at least at first. As time went on I began to pay closer attention to that man. I saw how friendly he was with the other kids, and something in me clicked. I can't say for sure what it was, other than a mother's intuition, but I felt it in my soul that he had something to do with the disappearance of my son. I didn't want to bring it to John and have him go out and get into trouble, so I prayed on it. I couldn't stand the sight of Father Fleming, so I found a church on the other side of town and went to confession one day to lay down my burdens."

"And what did you confess?" Detective Wolf asked.

"How much I hated Father Fleming. I was so mad that I wished death on him and anyone else that had been responsible for hurting my baby. I know it was wrong, but I couldn't hold that hate in. I had to let it out or it was going to consume me." Mrs. Gooden broke down in sobs.

"And then what happened?"

"The priest told me that God protected His flock and He would make things right, if I maintained my faith. When I got home I prayed harder than I had since Johnny went missing. I prayed the evil out of my heart and out of Father Fleming's. A few days later, the killings started."

"Why didn't you say something?"

"If you found out the man who had murdered your child was killed, would you complain?"

She had a point.

"Detective Wolf," she continued. "I know I was wrong for wishing death on those men, but you have to believe me when I say I never asked anyone to kill them."

"Still doesn't change the fact that people are dead and had you come forward we could've stopped it from going beyond Father Fleming."

"So what now? Are you going to arrest me?" Mrs. Gooden asked nervously.

"That was the plan when I came over here, but I don't think I will," Wolf said to her surprise.

"But those men—"

"Are dead, we've already established that. The man who killed your son got what he had coming to him as far as I'm concerned, and the rest, karma will settle up with eventually."

"So you're just going to let me go?" the woman asked in utter shock.

"Justice has already failed you once, Mrs. Gooden. Consider this just me balancing the scales. Give my best to your family, and enjoy the rest of your day." He left Mrs. Gooden standing there trying to figure out what had just happened.

Captain Marx sat outside at the little Italian bistro off Mulberry Street, enjoying the weather and a glass of red wine. It was late and most of the other diners had left. The bistro was one of his favorite spots and sometimes he stayed so late that he and the waitstaff were the only ones remaining. Since his retirement one month earlier, he'd spent most of his days building tiny ships inside bottles and reading books, and his nights soaking in the city. He was like a man in his second childhood.

Margaret Stone sauntered over to his table dressed in a low-cut black top and Capri pants. Diamonds flooded her neck and fingers, courtesy of her late husband's life insurance policy. She sat in the chair across from her brother, beaming.

"You're in an awfully good mood," Captain Marx observed.

"I am, and you should be too. The last payment was finally remitted to the Brotherhood. We are officially off the hook," she announced.

"Thank God," Marx sighed. "Now I can stop looking over my shoulder when I come out of the house. That was the longest thirty days of my life."

"Don't blame me, blame the government. If I had given them the entire million at one time, the IRS would've had a microscope shoved up my ass. I had to be resourceful."

"Well, as long as it's done, we can finally put all this nasty business behind us."

"Speaking of nasty business, how's our friend doing?" Margaret asked.

"Detective Sergeant Wolf is doing just what I said he would, enjoying that cushy little position and staying the hell out of my way."

"I still think I should've shot him too and let our secret die with him," Margaret said. She had initially planned on killing Wolf after she shot the Black Lotus, but the gun jammed. Had it not been for the police arriving before she could get it working, Detective Wolf would've been dead.

"Well, I'm glad you didn't. The kid is a headache, but I've still got a soft spot for him. I'm his daughter's godfather, for Christ's sake. You don't worry about Wolf, he's not going to be a problem for us."

At that moment the waitress came over. She was a short girl, with red hair and thick glasses. "Compliments of the chef," she said, setting two saucers on the table with small pieces of white chocolate cake topped with almonds.

"Tell Gino he's too kind, and this is for you, kid." Captain Marx slipped her a twenty-dollar bill. The waitress nodded in thanks and disappeared back inside the kitchen.

"I guess being a regular here has its perks," Margaret said before taking a bite of her cake. "My goodness, this is delicious! Aren't you going to try it?"

"Nah, my diabetes has been kicking up lately," Captain Marx responded. "But you enjoy."

The brother and sister made light conversation while she ate cake and he sipped wine. She was in the process of telling him about an office space she was thinking about moving into when her face suddenly went slack.

"What's wrong?" Marx asked.

Margaret tried to speak, but it was like she couldn't catch her breath. She fell from her chair and began to convulse violently, foaming at the mouth.

Marx dropped to his knees and began shaking her. "Margaret? Margaret! Oh my God, someone get some help!" he screamed. The busboy who had been clearing off a table next to them simply walked away as if he didn't even see them. "What the hell is going on?"

"Looks like the arsenic I laced her almonds with is kicking in." The redheaded waitress was standing over them. He hadn't even heard her approach. "I'd planned on both of you eating the cake and making this less messy, but I guess I have to improvise." She picked up a steak knife from the next table.

The captain looked up in shock. It only took him a few seconds to process what was happening. The whole time he had been looking for a man to come at him, though he had been mistaken. "But I don't understand . . . We gave the Brotherhood a million dollars to call you off."

"I'm no dog of the Brotherhood. I am the hand of God and the harbinger of justice," she said venomously.

"I'll kill you!" Marx sprang to his feet and charged at her.

The redhead sidestepped him, slicing the knife through his belly. Without breaking her motion, she cut him across his back before bringing the knife around in an arc and embedding it in his collar. With a yank, she hacked through flesh and muscle, breaking the blade off when it made contact with his spinal cord.

Captain Marx clutched at his wound futilely, hands slick with blood. As he fell he reached for the woman, managing to grab her hair. The red wig slid off her head, revealing the mane of thick black hair hiding beneath. A light of recognition went off in his eyes, because he had seen his killer's face before—at the crime scene where Poncho was killed, then again when he reviewed the footage from Margaret's ribbon-cutting ceremony. She was the reporter asking the uncomfortable questions. He opened his mouth to curse her, but all that came out was a sick gurgling sound.

Kahllah stood there watching as the light drained from Captain Marx's eyes. His death was a slow and painful one, which made her smile. "Little Johnny Gooden sends his regards from the grave," she spat on his dead body. From the pocket of her apron she produced two black lotuses and placed one on each corpse. "And for a time evil was still and the night was again quiet," she said, before vanishing just as suddenly as she had come.

THE END

ALSO BY K'WAN

Gangsta, 2002

Horse, 2002

The Game (Anthology), 2003

Road Dawgz, 2003

Street Dreams, 2004

Hoodlum, 2005

Eve, 2006

Hood Rat (Book 1), 2006

"A Hood Rat Short" (Free Story), 2007

Still Hood (Book 2), 2007

Blow, 2007

Flexin & Sexin (Anthology), 2007

From the Streets to the Sheets (Anthology), 2008

"Gangsta Walk" (Free Story), 2008

Gutter, 2008

Law & Order (Free Story), 2009

Section 8 (Book 3), 2009

Flirt (Anthology), 2009

"The Leak" (Free Short), 2010

Welfare Wifeys (Book 4), 2010

From Harlem with Love, 2010

Eviction Notice (Book 5), 2011

Love & Gunplay (Book 5.5), 2012

Animal (Book 6), 2012

Purple Reign, 2013

Animal 2: The Omen, 2013

Little Nikki Grind, 2014

The Fix, 2014

ALSO AVAILABLE FROM INFAMOUS BOOKS

H.N.I.C.
BY **ALBERT "PRODIGY" JOHNSON**
WITH **STEVEN SAVILE**

128 PAGES, HARDCOVER $19.95, TRADE PAPER, $11.95, E-BOOK, $4.99

Prodigy, from the legendary hip-hop group Mobb Deep, launches Akashic's Infamous Books imprint with a story of loyalty, vengeance, and greed.

"The work is a breath of fresh air from lengthy, trying-too-hard-to-shock street lit and is an excellent choice for all metropolitan collections."
—*Library Journal* (**Starred Review and Pick of the Month**)

THE WHITE HOUSE
BY **JaQUAVIS COLEMAN**

112 PAGES, HARDCOVER $19.95, TRADE PAPER, $11.95, E-BOOK, $4.99

One house ... one robbery ... one mistake ... Sexual intrigue and violence intermingle in this tense urban thriller.

JaQuavis Coleman is the *New York Times* best-selling author of Dopeman's Trilogy.

SWING
BY **MIASHA**

160 PAGES, HARDCOVER $19.95, TRADE PAPER, $11.95, E-BOOK, $4.99

An erotic drama about four sexy couples and one swingers' club where their fantasies and nightmares collide.

"Miasha is a writer to watch."
—*Publishers Weekly*